MW00479981

THE LESSONS OF LABRADORS

A Love & Pets Romantic Comedy, Book 4

A.G. HENLEY

No part of this book may be reproduced in any form or by any electronic or mechanical means, including information storage and retrieval systems, without written permission from the author, except for the use of brief quotations in a book review.

This is a work of fiction. Names, characters, places, and incidents are the product of the author's imagination or are used fictitiously. Any resemblance to actual person, living or dead, events, or locales is entirely coincidental.

Copyright © 2020 by A.G. Henley

Cover Designed by Najla Qamber Designs (www.najlaqamberdesigns.com)

All rights reserved by A.G. Henley

Visit me at aghenley.com

Summary: A woman joins a pet grief support group and finds a second chance at love.

CONTENTS

Hey, readers!

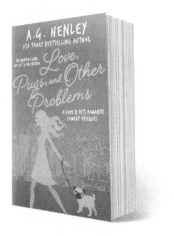

Get the FREE prequel ebook to the Love & Pets series, *Love, Pugs, and Other Problems,* an exclusive short story that tells how Amelia gets Doug the pug instead of a ring! Go to aghenley.com/free-books.

Chapter One

Sarah
Lost Paws, Session One

I take a seat in the circle of chairs in the basement meeting room of Most Glorious Blood of Christ Catholic Church and watch nervously as other group members make their way in. I'm clutching the framed picture of Sam that I'd spent an embarrassing amount of time selecting.

A few faded religious posters hang on the walls of the sparsely furnished room, and thin industrial carpet lines the floor. A whiteboard is at the head of the circle next to an empty chair. The room looks like . . . the basement meeting room of any one of thousands of churches around the United States.

I wasn't sure what to expect when I signed up for a pet grief support group, and to be honest, I'm still not sure I made the right decision to come.

It's Tuesday night, one of my few evenings off from the library, and I have a lot of adulting to do. But as my best friend

Angela told me, if I don't climb back onto the train of life, it's going to pass me by . . . and royally screw up my hair as it goes. I take a deep breath. I can do this.

A middle-aged woman with dark blonde hair swept up in a pile on her head comes my way wearing an empathic smile. Although it's the last day of March in Colorado—which means it's flipping freezing—she's wearing capri pants, hiking-style sandals with socks, and a white T-shirt featuring a screen-printed photograph of an equally blonde cocker spaniel. The resemblance between the dog and the T-shirt wearer is seriously uncanny.

The woman greets me, her voice warm. "I'm Bev Philson, the leader of the Lost Paws group. May I see your fur baby?"

With a small smile, I hold out the picture of Sam for her.

"Oh, a yellow Labrador retriever!" she says. "What wonderful, loyal dogs they are. You must be . . . Sarah Newsome?"

Wow, Bev read my sign-up form thoroughly. I nod and stand to shake her outstretched hand. She grabs mine with both of hers and pumps it up and down.

"So nice to meet you. Thank you for joining the group. We'll get started in a few minutes."

I settle myself back in my chair, swiping at the chocolate curls that fall in my eyes whenever I move my head, as Bev greets the woman in the plain metal chair next to me.

My neighbor has salt-and-pepper hair pulled back in a low bun, she wears all black from head to toe, a large silver cross hangs at her neck, and a framed image of a massive Saint Bernard rests on her knees. The dog looks friendly in a slobbery sort of way. The older woman smells like baby powder, which reminds me of my grandmother back in Omaha.

Bev greets her and oohs and aahs over the dog before moving on to the twenty-something man slouching in a chair across the circle, no pet picture in sight. His jeans are full of holes, and his metal band sweatshirt has paint stains on it. I think he was staring at my boobs a minute ago.

Next to him, an African American woman talks with an older Latino man. They have pictures, too. I'm relieved to see I'm not the only fool clutching a picture of my dead dog.

I'm preparing to eavesdrop on Bev's conversation with the others when I catch sight of a new guy walking in. My mouth drops open, and my breath catches.

He wears jeans, a pale-green button-down shirt, and loafers. His brown hair is shorter than it used to be, and his eyes are a gorgeous shade of spring green and fall gold.

I know, because I stared at them often enough back in college when he would come into the library where I'd worked part-time.

Ben Becker. It's been six years since I've seen him, but he still looks good enough to eat with whipped cream and sprinkles. My heart, cold and still for the last six months, unexpectedly pumps. Probably feeling me staring at him like a cat that found a bird lunching on its scratching post, Ben glances at me.

I look away. I won't give him the satisfaction of showing him I remember him. Not after the way we'd ended things. I turn instead to Bev, who sits in the empty chair at the front after briefly greeting Ben. She beams at each of us in turn.

"Good evening, everyone, and welcome to our first session! This is Lost Paws, the pet grief support group. If you're here for Celibrate—the support group that celebrates celibacy—it's on Saturday nights at nine o'clock. An excellent day and time for it, don't you think?"

She stops, waiting for us to laugh. I smile uncomfortably and avoid looking anywhere near Ben. Which isn't easy—he's sitting across from me, next to the slouchy guy.

Bev composes her face and her tone takes a serious turn. "We're all here because we've lost someone close to us."

My gut clenches. I will *not* cry in the first minute of the group session. The older woman beside me digs in her purse and pulls out a tissue. I pat her back, and she offers me a watery smile. At least I won't be the first one to leak.

"That includes me." Bev pulls her shirt out from her chest so we can see the cocker spaniel better. "This is Adorabelle—Belle —my fur baby who crossed over the Rainbow Bridge nearly ten years ago now."

No. Please. Not the Rainbow Bridge again. Sam's waiting for me there, or so my neighbor and good friend Rose Bush tells me. And yes, that's her actual name.

I prefer to think of Sam lounging on a couch made of clouds, lunching on as many Vienna sausages as he can before ambling down a wide mountain path with tons of chipmunks to chase. Now that would be his idea of heaven, not some bridge made of water and light.

"My own struggle to heal my broken heart after Belle's death is what led me to start Lost Paws," Bev says. "I'm a licensed professional counselor, trained right here in Fort Collins. I completed my graduate degree through Colorado State University's Department of Psychology."

I have an even harder time not sneaking a peek at Ben. CSU is our alma mater, too.

"I have a private practice focusing on helping older folks with food fetishes," Bev says, "but I save one night a week for this group. It holds a special place in my heart."

The African American woman and I exchange an *um, okay* look. Talk about a niche.

Bev picks up a piece of paper from her chair. "Now, before we get to know each other better, I'd like to lay out the ground rules for the group. First, like in Las Vegas, what happens in the group stays in the group. That's everything from information as basic as our names to things shared in session." She gives us a stern look. "Confidentiality is essential to any therapeutic endeavor.

"Second, please try to be on time and attend all sessions. Healing only happens if you're here, friends." She beams at us.

"Third, no talking about group members when they aren't in group. No one likes to be talked about behind their back, do they? And fourth, no socializing outside of group. Friendly inter-actions before or after group is acceptable, of course, but friend-ships should wait at least until group concludes on May nineteenth." I again avoid Ben's eyes as Bev pauses. "Any questions?"

The sloucher raises his hand. "Has anyone, like, hooked up with someone in the group before?" He glances at me and cocks an eyebrow.

I wince. Please tell me the first man under sixty to be inter-ested in me in months is not the one who looks like he rolled out of the Narcotics Anonymous group that's probably here on Monday nights to confess their weekend sins. The patrons of the library skew towards elderly, and I've had my fair share of being hit on by baby boomers with too much Viagra on their hands.

"I'm sure it's happened," Bev says, "but not until after the group ended." She claps her hands. "Okay, I know it can be a little stressful to speak in front of a group of strangers, so we'll do an icebreaking exercise with a partner first." She holds up three fingers and wiggles them around. Gold rings wink from several digits. "I'd like you and your partner to share three things about yourself: your name, your pet's name, and the thing you miss the most about them."

Crap. I'm going to cry for sure. But it's time to tear the Band-Aid off, I guess. I turn to the woman next to me as Bev adds, "Why don't you pair up with the person sitting directly across from you?"

The sloucher across the circle grins like he's won a free year of Playboy TV, while the smile I was in the process of painting on starts to drip. It gets worse when Ben jumps up and heads my way with a smile and a raised eyebrow.

"Hey, partner."

Okay, he *could* have been my knight in organic cotton and selvage denim. Except that, six years ago, he lied and broke my heart.

The panic sets in again. I'm partnering with Ben Becker, my

gorgeous ex-boyfriend—if you can call someone you only went out with a handful of times that—while blubbering uncontrollably about Sam.

On second thought, give me the slouch.

Chapter Two

Sarah

Reluctantly, I give my chair to the now annoyed-looking sloucher, and move with Ben back to his side of the circle. The Hispanic man and African American woman pair up.

I do my best to not fidget with my sweater as I sit beside Ben. I have a long-standing, unconscious habit of arranging my tops to ensure my 36E chest is tastefully covered. Flaunt it, Angela would tell me. Easy for her to say. She's a perfect hourglass.

I'm determined not to speak first, so I stare at the board as if I've forgotten what the three things were. Only, they aren't written on the board. So now I just look weird.

"Sarah? You're Sarah Newsome, right?" Ben smiles at me. "I don't know if you remember me, but we were friends in college. I'm Ben Becker."

Remember him? Friends? Ben was like my graduation gift from the CSU gods. He came into my library day after day, doing research for a senior paper in engineering, and torturing me with his politeness and good looks. When he finally asked me out for coffee, I knew my life was going to be champagne and roses from then on.

And it did go well at first. But then . . . heartbreak.

I smile grimly. "I remember."

His forehead scrunches; he probably senses my unfriendliness. It would be a lot easier to be unfriendly if he didn't smell so wonderful, like coffee-scented shaving cream.

"You look great." His eyes manage to take me in without making me feel like I'm a slice of extra thick cheesecake he's about to dig into.

"Thanks," I say.

I'd cut my hair and learned how to dress to fit my curvy figure since college. I'm not Instagram-influencer skinny now— not by a long shot—but I make it a priority to eat right and exercise to maintain a healthy weight for me. While still enjoying the occasional pint of ice cream or the odd box of Girl Scout cookies.

Mmm, thinking about that last box of Tagalongs at home makes my mouth water. Sam and I used to share a box together. Not Tagalongs, of course, they have chocolate. But Do-Si-Dos, Trefoils, and the like were fair game.

"So, what are you up to now?" Ben asks.

"Tagalongs," I say. When his brow furrows, I realize I'd said that out loud. "Oh! I'm a librarian for the city and county of Fort Collins."

He smiles, like he's really interested. "Yeah? Which one?"

"Old Town."

"That's a great little library. Love the neighborhood."

It's the neighborhood where I live now, but I don't volunteer that.

"What about you?" I strive to sound utterly disinterested, but I doubt I'm successful. Disinterested isn't really my style. I'm usually like a puppy, practically rolling all over to show my interest in new people.

"I'm a software engineer. I went to Boulder for graduate school and now I work for a company based in Denver with a satellite office here in Fort Collins."

So he went to our rivals, University of Colorado, after college. I'd stayed at CSU for my master's degree in library science.

"Take another minute to wrap up," Bev says from beside the African American woman and her partner. Ben raises his eyebrows.

"I guess we'd better do the assignment," he says. "I know your name. So, who was your pet and what do you miss most about him or her?"

I'm still holding Sam's picture, so I show it to Ben. "This guy. Sam."

And as if on cue, my eyes start to water. I've had involuntary eyeball salt baths every day since Sam passed away in my arms, euthanized in my living room by my wonderful and compassionate veterinarian Dr. Travis Brewer and his assistant Amelia of Love & Pets Mobile Animal Clinic.

Noooo! Don't cry in front of the ex-boyfriend who broke your heart after only a few dates!

Ben's face pinches with sympathy as I search the pockets of my royal-blue cardigan for the wad of tissues I'd stuffed in there before I got here. Ben steps to the small table next to Bev's chair and grabs a box of tissues for me.

I swipe a few and wipe my cheeks. I hate that I'm crying in front of him, but honestly? I've cried in front of everyone I know in the past few months.

I still can't believe Sam is gone. He was my buddy, my companion, my fur baby for a too-short six years. He was my blanket on movie nights, my greeter each and every time I came home, my walking partner. I took him everywhere I possibly could and even places I shouldn't have, like my Aunt Teresa's house. She's a fur Nazi.

I just can't seem to get past Sam's death. I think about him constantly. I miss him. I'm here because I need to heal the Sam-sized hole in my heart.

"It still feels like it was yesterday," I say, while also trying to make sure I don't miss any snot coming out of my nose, "and the thing I miss most since he's been gone is how he used to greet me when I got home. It was like I was his long-lost best friend, gone for years, every single day. I hate the silence now."

No whines or woofs of hello as I open the door, no tail wags, no nudging me toward his leash hanging in the coat closet or toward his food bowl after our walk. Only the plodding tick of the antique grandfather clock Rose gifted me from her side of the duplex last year.

"When did he die?" Ben asks softly. His arm is draped over the back of my chair. Oh, no you don't. You don't get to play nice now, Mister Liar, Liar, Pants on Fire.

"About six months ago." I blow my nose, doing my best to make sure I don't wipe off all my makeup in the process. "He had leukemia. I, I've had a hard time getting over it, you know?"

I sniff and swipe at my face one last time with a clean tissue. "You'd better tell me about your pet. We're going to run out of time."

Ben glances away, but not before I see what looks like pain etched on his handsome features. Huh, maybe the old Apple of My Lie has a heart now. Maybe.

"His name was Bailey when he was good, Failey when he was bad, and Snailey as he got old." Ben smiles, but his eyes narrow with contained emotion. "He was a dog like any other dog, but he was ours."

Ours? As in his and hers? Probably. Did I think "Gone in the Blink of a Lie" Becker would still be single? I have no time to ask him. Bev takes her seat, and we all quiet down.

"Now," she says, "I'd like you to introduce your partner and their pet to the group. Who would like to start?"

Everyone looks around shyly. The African American woman raises her hand. "I'll go."

"This is Oscar," she nods at the Latino man, who smiles. He has chubby cheeks covered in gray stubble, and he's wearing jeans, old running shoes, and a navy canvas jacket with his name embroidered on it.

"He lost his cat, Baloney. He and his wife still have Baloney's sister, Cheese, but . . . they both miss the meat that made the sandwich good." She says it like she's quoting what he told her. We all laugh.

"Can you show the group the picture you brought of Baloney?" Bev asks. Oscar holds up a grainy unframed shot of a black blur. He shrugs. "He didn't sit still much."

"Welcome to the group, Oscar. I'm so sorry for your loss of sweet Baloney," Bev says.

Oscar's belly shakes with laughter, although I see him swipe his cheek quickly. "Oh, Baloney wasn't sweet. He was *un tigre*. But my wife Edith and me, we loved him."

He gestures to his partner. "This is Patricia. She lost her poodle called Snickerdoodle—"

"Or Snickerpoodle." Patricia smiles sadly.

"And she misses how her dog would put her head under her arm when she'd been holding her phone for too long and push it up." He looks at his partner for confirmation.

Patricia nods. "Sometimes she made me accidentally throw it, but I didn't mind. It was a good reminder to get off Facebook, stop watching Netflix, or whatever other nonsense I was wasting time doing, and pay attention to her."

"Welcome, Patricia," Bev says. "I'm very sorry about Snicker-doodle." She turns to the slouch and the older woman. He jerks a thumb at his partner.

"This is Lydia. Her dog was a Saint Bernard named Sister Mary Margaret."

Lydia crosses herself. She's holding a rosary now along with the picture of the dog.

The guy goes on. "She misses how, um, Sister would pray with her every night."

Lydia nods fervently. Then, her chin tips to her chest and she begins sobbing. The young guy looks flummoxed. My own eyes water again as Bev rushes to Lydia's side to offer her a fresh box of tissue.

To his credit, the slouch holds the picture of Sister Mary Margaret that his partner thrusted at him when she started crying. As for me, I'm mostly glad I'm not the only one who might cry their way through all eight sessions.

I sniffle and wipe my eyes again. Ben touches my back, and as much as I want to elbow him or shoot him a nasty look, instead, I have a hard time not leaning into him like I might have with Sam. Ben is not a dog. Ben is not a dog.

Lydia doesn't stop crying, although it's gotten softer now. Bev looks at the slouch, who stood to let her sit beside the older woman. "Do you mind introducing yourself?"

He pulls the bottom hem of his hoodie up around his neck as if to take it off. He's not wearing a shirt on underneath.

"What are you doing?" Bev asks. Even Lydia's crying slows as she stares.

"Showing you my pet." He tugs the sweatshirt off. A tattoo of a thick, dark snake encircles his chest, shoulders, and, I assume, his back. The serpent's head lays on the man's heart. The name Severus is tattooed under it.

"I'm Brent, and my snake Sev died about two months ago, and I can't ... I don't know ... I can't stop thinking about him. I miss him. He was a real chick magnet when I went out."

The rest of us laugh, a little uncomfortably.

"What kind of snake was it?" Patricia asks with a shudder.

"A boa constrictor. Sev was beautiful. His pattern was the coolest I'd ever seen." He shuffles his feet. "And now, I keep thinking he's still around. Like, I hear him moving at night in his terrarium, but when I go to check, it's empty like always."

I try to look sympathetic, but a quick glance around tells me everyone looks about as weirded out as I feel. How can someone get that worked up about a dead snake?

"Welcome to the group, Brent," Bev says. "I'm sorry to hear about Severus." Bev gets up to give Brent his seat back and looks at me and Ben Becker, also known as old Leave Her High and Lie.

"And how about you two?"

Chapter Three

Ben

I introduce Sarah to the group. I could share a lot more about her than what she's told me. I remember almost everything about this woman, although I wouldn't tell her that right now. Not unless I wanted her to think I was a stalker *and* a liar.

I reach for Sam's picture. "This is Sarah's Labrador retriever, Sam. She misses how he was always excited to see her when she got home."

The other dog owners in the group nod and smile at me.

I'd met Sarah at the library where she worked; we'd flirted for a couple months before I'd finally asked her out for coffee. But there was the whole thing with my ex-girlfriend, Alexa, and by the time I'd gotten everything straightened out, Sarah wouldn't speak to me. Plus, I'd moved to Denver to start a new job, the only one I'd had before going back to grad school. But I hadn't forgotten about Sarah. Not for a second.

Now here she is. And here I am. This could be my chance to

reconnect with the girl who I genuinely thought would be my first serious girlfriend after college.

Except now I have a problem. A Pinocchio-sized problem.

"Welcome, Sarah," Bev says. "I'm sorry for your loss."

Sarah nods and gestures to me. "This is Ben. His dog was Bailey. Or Failey, or Snailey. And . . ." Her forehead wrinkles, and she looks at me. "And I forgot to ask what you miss most about him."

I scramble for an answer.

"How, uh, how fun he was. We had a great time together."

"Do you have a picture?" Bev asks.

I hold up my hands. "I forgot it . . . but I can describe him. Bailey was a black Lab. Not a big, powerful one; he was on the smaller side. But he was an awesome dog."

Sarah's blue eyes watch me closely while I talk. I'll bet she senses there's more to my story. And she's right, but I'll never be able to tell her what it is.

Bev welcomes me to the group. "I'm sorry for your loss of Bailey."

I nod and lean back in my chair, happy to be off the witness stand. Bev gets up and addresses the group.

"Processing grief is very personal. We don't all do it the same way. And it's just that—a process. It's not a race, it's not a task to be checked off your to-do list, it's not a battle to be won. It's something you must commit to feeling and experiencing. And grieving a pet is sometimes even harder than grieving a person because not everyone around us understands."

I nod, thinking of my friends after Bailey died. They'd been cool about it, but I could tell they hadn't understood why I wouldn't get over it already.

"So, let's start with talking about the Kübler-Ross model of the stages of grief."

Bev walks to a whiteboard on the wall where her name and the group's names are. Beside it, she writes the words *denial, anger, bargaining, depression, and acceptance* in a circle. Inside the circle, she draws arrows moving from one word to the next, but also from each word to all the other words in a star shape.

"The old way of thinking was that you start at denial," she points to the word, "and move from that stage to the next predictably," her finger slides to anger, "like—what do the kids say?—leveling your way up through a video game."

She shakes her head. "That's not how it works. The stages are merely helpful concepts. You might start in one stage, like anger, and instead of inevitably moving on to bargaining, you slide back to denial, then skip up to depression, and never experience bargaining. That's okay, that's to be expected . . ."

She goes on talking about what grieving people might be feeling. Sadness, anger, bitterness, disbelief, loneliness. "You might be angry at a partner who didn't want to pay for further expensive treatment for your pet. You might be angry at the veterinarian who you felt might not have given your pet the kind of care you thought they deserved. You might even be angry at God."

Lydia raises a pale hand.

"Yes?" Bev asks.

The older woman coughs lightly. When she speaks, she has an accent. Irish, I think. "One must never be angry with God. One must believe that He is all-knowing and all-seeing, while our sight is weak and poor in comparison."

Bev's mouth opens, but she doesn't seem to know what to say. Lydia takes her silence as an invitation to carry on.

"When my Sister Mary Margaret became ill," she crosses herself, "I put her life in God's hands, knowing that He would provide."

My eyebrow rises a little. And look how that turned out. I catch Sarah glancing at me, and I realize I'm smirking. I straighten my face quickly.

Oscar raises a hand. "Does grief make you hungry? I've been eating all the time ever since Baloney died." He puts his hands on his stomach. "My Edith says I'm filling the hole he left in my heart with *comida*."

Bev starts to speak, but Brent beats her to it. "I don't know, man, I've lost weight. Every time I go in the fridge to get something to eat, I see Sev's rats, and I get, like, sad."

Patricia draws back, a hand on her suit collar. She's dressed better by far than the rest of us. "You have *rats* in your refrigerator?"

Brent shrugs. "In the freezer, yeah."

"*Frozen* rats?" Patricia says.

Lydia fingers her rosary and mutters a prayer or incantation or something.

"That's what Sev ate." Brent spreads his hands out, palms up. "Snake, remember?"

We all wear similar expressions of disgust. I ask what I guess we're all thinking. "If he's, er, passed on, why don't you throw the rats out?"

Brent smooths his jeans. "They were expensive. And I might get another snake."

Bev takes the opportunity to jump in. "This is my point. We all will experience grief in different ways. Oscar feels hungry while Brent doesn't have much of an appetite. Lydia takes comfort in her faith—"

Lydia makes a distressed noise and dabs at her eyes with a tissue. Bev puts on what I'm starting to think of as her therapist face: lips thinned in an understanding smile, forehead wrinkled, nodding to show she gets you.

Only, Bev's comment must have touched a nerve because now Lydia's full-on sobbing, and before I know it, so is Sarah. I want to put an arm around her, but it feels inappropriate. So, I reach over and pat her back kind of awkwardly.

I throw a desperate look at Bev. She has her hands full with Lydia, so I keep patting Sarah until she finally stops crying. Oh, crap. Even with a red and blotchy face, she's still pretty.

Sarah pats her face with a clean tissue. "I'm sorry."

I shake my head. "For what? Feeling something?"

She tilts her head. "I guess?"

"Don't. Don't apologize for being human."

She smiles, and I cringe inside. Way to be patronizing, Ben. And who are you to give advice on anything having to do with grief? I push my lips together. I shouldn't be here. This is wrong, wrong, wrong.

The thing is, I'd just planned to come to this one group. I'm only here at all because I lost a poker hand to my brother, Adam. He'd said if I couldn't cover my bet, which I couldn't, I had to do whatever he said. And like a dope, I'd agreed.

He'd consulted a community calendar and originally told me I had to crash the group that celebrates celibacy. Uh, no. So, I'd looked at the list and picked this one. I thought I'd come once, satisfy the debt, and then I'd be gone.

But now—Sarah is here. Sarah, who seems as cool, kind, and gorgeous as she'd been back in college. Before she thought I'd lied about still being with Alexa. Which, for the record, I hadn't. Sarah, who I haven't been able to get out of my head completely since then.

Maybe I could get to know her again. Maybe even have another shot with her. Except ... this time I'm lying for real.

Here's the deal: I did have a dog named Bailey whom I loved. And my friends hadn't totally gotten it when I was sad after he died.

Because we had all been nine years old.

I should tell Sarah the truth. Today. Now. Or at least right after group. I imagine our conversation:

Sarah, it's good to see you again. Hey, so I'm not really grieving because I haven't had a dog in twenty years. I actually have bad pet allergies. Why am I here? Good question ... Because I'm a terrible person who doesn't mind exploiting people who are at a low point in their lives in order to cover a betting loss in a friendly poker game with my brother and some buddies. So—wanna go for a beer?

I can't tell her that. She clearly remembers what happened in college. Admitting that I'm crashing a group of grieving pet owners would destroy any thought in her head that I might be more mature and trustworthy at age twenty-eight than I was at twenty-two.

I'm not risking it; I'm staying in the group.

I can let this play out for a while and tell her later. She'll forgive me once she has a chance to get to know me again.

Even if it was decades ago, I had lost Bailey. Time doesn't heal all wounds, after all. It didn't cure me of Sarah.

Chapter Four

Sarah

"So then, Lydia and I burst into ugly, snotty tears right in front of everyone, and the next thing you know, Ben's patting my back and comforting me."

"Who's Lydia again?" Angela asks from the dressing room.

"The older lady with the Saint Bernard."

"Who makes the sign of the cross every time she says the dog's name, right?"

"That's the one."

Behind the heavy cream curtain, my best friend and library partner in crime tries on her fifth wedding dress of the hour. She's marrying her fiancé, Julian, in exactly six weeks, and I'm her maid of honor. She's a little behind on the planning, so she really does need to pick a dress tonight.

I play with the tassel of the cream-colored fancy silk pillow I'm cradling. I'm sitting in an overstuffed, white-as-snow chair in the corner of the dressing room at The Quick and the Wed, winner of Fort Collin's coolest—and most humorously titled—

bridal shop. Everything in the room is white, cream, or gold, except the tremendous pink and white arrangement of lilies artfully placed on a round table in the middle of the room. I feel like I'm lounging on a layer of someone's wedding cake.

As I wait for Ang to emerge and show off the next dress, I relive afresh the horror of bursting into tears at Lost Paws two nights before. It was just that when I was upset, Sam had given me the same kind of compassionate look that Bev gave Lydia. He'd stop whatever he was doing, tilt his head to the side, and touch his nose to my chest as if to say he understood I was hurting. And that he hurt because I did. Because we were family.

But . . . I can't believe I'd lost it like that in front of Ben. And the rest of the group. But mostly Ben.

Is there a stage of grief called humiliation?

"What did Ben say?" Ang asks.

"I don't know. I was too mortified. I think he was actually kind of sweet about it." I put my head in my hands. "I'd managed to not blubber while I was talking to him, and then I thought of Sam, and I couldn't hold in the tears. It was inexorable."

"I mean, he sounds okay. What was his crime back in college?"

I remember every detail, so it's no problem to tell her. It only hurts a little anymore. Ben and I had met at the library. He'd come in to find books that he later admitted he didn't need, and I'd found excuses to shelve books in the section where he studied that didn't need to be shelved.

Finally, he'd asked me out on a date, and another, and then another.

"He took me to a rare book festival, a performance of *Evita* at the Denver Center, and to coffee, right around the corner at Alleycat." He was such a good guy, or so I'd thought at the time.

"Sounds like things were going fine. What happened?" Ang asks.

I sigh. "He lied." I think about the painful moment when I'd realized I couldn't trust Ben. "We were out at a restaurant, and he went to the restroom and left his phone on the table."

"Uh-oh," comes from the dressing room.

"Yeah," I say.

"Did you snoop?" Ang asks.

"No! I wouldn't do that." Usually. "A text from his ex-girl-friend, Alexa Parker, showed up on his lock screen. He'd told me he'd broken up with her a few weeks before he asked me out the first time. But she didn't sound like she knew they weren't together anymore."

"What did the text say?"

"I can't repeat it in polite company."

"Whoever called me polite?" There's a thump and a mild curse from the dressing room.

"You okay?"

"Yeah, I fell against the wall trying to get my heels on. What did you do when Ben came out of the bathroom?"

"Confronted him! He made up some story about Alexa not letting things go, but he seemed nervous and shady about it. I thanked him for dinner and left. *Before* I ate."

"That's character, right there."

"Right?" I say before taking a swig of my Diet Coke. "He tried to call me a few times after that, but I know a lie when I hear one."

"Well, that was college," Ang says. "I'd hate for people to judge me on everything *I* did back then."

I nod to myself. "True."

"If he's a decent guy now, he won't hold a snotty cry against you, no matter how inexorable." She pulls the curtain aside.

I gasp. "Oh, Ang. I love that one. You look stunning."

My friend smooths the lace bodice and steps in front of the lighted, three-panel mirror of the dressing room. "I love it. But will Julian like it?"

My gaze moves from the plunging yet still decorous neckline, past Angela's perfectly proportioned curves, to the shimmery hem at her feet. "Julian will not be able to take his eyes—or his hands—off of you in that dress."

"That's the idea," Angela twirls in front of the mirror looking every inch of the Haitian American goddess that she is. Her dark skin shows to perfection against the white material.

I gesture to the lineup of gowns I carefully hung on a rack after Ang tried them on. "I can't wait to see you walking down that aisle in one of these. Let me see the front again." She turns to me.

"I love it. I think this one is my favorite."

"You've said that about every dress!"

I grimace. "I can't decide! You look fabulous in all of them."

"That's wonderful, but I need help *choosing*. One more to try." Angela disappears back inside the dressing room.

I've been the maid of honor in six weddings since college, at least one each year since I graduated. And Angela's wedding, while especially special, isn't the only one I'm in this year.

My neighbor and friend Rose is marrying her beau, Charles, a few weeks after Ang and Julian wed. Guess who she asked to be her maid of honor? She only has a son, and she doesn't like her daughter-in-law.

Lucky me.

I chide myself for thinking that. I'm thrilled and honored to have been asked by not one but two wonderful women whom I love. I only wish I could see the chance, the inkling, the minute possibility of starring in the main event myself. But alas, always the bridesmaid . . . You know the rest.

Angela shows me the next dress, one with a much fuller skirt and too low-cut in the back. She picks up on the fact that I don't like it as much, so she changes back to her own clothes.

"Okay, which one?" she asks.

"They were all amazing."

"Which one, Sarah!"

I bite my lip, scan the options on the rack, and pick the second to last dress she tried on. "You actually glowed in it."

"I loved it, too." She squeals and hugs me. "I found a dress!" She pulls her coat on and checks her watch. "I'm so sorry to wedding dress and run, but Julian's meeting me outside."

"Where are you two going?"

She checks her hair in the mirror. "Dinner at L'Orange."

"Ah, the life you do lead. Wedding dresses followed by cocktails and dinner with the love of your life."

"Ha, more like water with lemon and a salad. I've got six weeks to fit into that dress the way it's meant to be worn." Ang puts her hands on my arms. "You know you're always welcome to join us."

I hug her again. "I know. But I have a hot date myself with leftovers and the next episode of *Love in the Sand*."

She groans. "You're still watching that series? It's so corny. All those couples meeting at the beach and making each other's dreams come true."

"I like corn."

"Don't I know it, too. It's time you found your own patch of sand, along with a hot waiter or lifeguard or surfer—"

I quirk an eyebrow. "In Fort Collins? We're landlocked."

Angela takes my hand as we walk to the front of the shop. "Seriously, I like the sound of this Ben guy. Why don't you ask him to meet you for coffee or something?"

"Can't. It's against the group rules."

Ang hands the dress she selected to the salesperson and lets her know she'll be back for a proper fitting in the next few days. It was a minor miracle that we got the woman to leave us alone with the dresses without her hovering.

My friend makes a face as we step outside. "Are you really going to let some lame rule stop you from having coffee with someone?"

I pull my scarf up to my chin against the early evening chill. "The group just started, and I already made a total fool of myself. I don't want to break rules now, too."

She puts an arm around me. "Always the good girl."

I pretend to be offended. "No, I'm not. Remember when we were up at Strawberry Park Hot Springs? I wore my bathing suit in the birthday-suit-only pool."

She laughs, dazzling me with her perfect smile. "You're such a rebel." She looks behind me, and her eyes light up. "Hey, babe."

I turn to greet Julian. He looks as handsome as ever in well-fitting slacks with a midnight-blue wool winter coat and a perfectly arranged gray cashmere scarf. He wears a trimmed mustache and goatee, while the rest of his dark skin is smooth. I glance down at my own scarf. It's like someone tried to strangle me with it. I can never get them to look right. I busy myself with pulling gloves on while my friend thoroughly kisses her fiancé.

Julian pecks me on the cheek after they come up for air. "Hey, MOH." He's taken to calling me maid of honor—MOH for short. He has an amazing, rich voice that would make movie trailer voice-over guys envious.

Ang wraps her hand around her fiancé's upper arm. "Sarah met someone!"

"Who? Where? And doing what?" His eyebrows bounce suggestively.

"In my support group," I say. "And it's nothing. He's an old college friend."

"An old college lover," Ang says.

"Really?" Julian looks intrigued.

"Hardly. We went on a few dates." Before I realized Ben was a Far Lie from honest.

"But now the former lovers meet again, united in pet grief," Ang says dramatically. "Wait, what is he grieving?"

"His black Lab, Bailey."

"He's a Lab lover? You didn't mention that part," Ang says.

"Ben also said Bailey was his and someone else's, which I assume means a girlfriend or partner."

He hadn't been wearing a wedding ring, but I can't imagine someone as handsome as him would be single. That's not physically possible at our age, so far as I can tell. The really good-looking ones are either taken, cheating, or jerks.

"You know what they say about *assume*," Ang says.

"What?" I ask.

She thinks about it. "That you shouldn't do it."

Julian laughs. "Well said, babe."

"You sure you don't want to join us for dinner?" Ang asks me.

"No, thanks. You two go ahead."

I watch them walk away, hand in hand, my heart aching. Don't get me wrong; I'm incredibly happy for them. Angela has had her fair share of heartaches, too.

But as I head for my car and my lonely duplex, I wonder, When will I get my happy ending?

Chapter Five

Sarah

I watch my breath curl into the crisp spring air as I walk to my car. Fort Collins is nestled next to the foothills of the Rocky Mountains between hip Boulder and cowboy-cool Wyoming. It's still a small city, but it's growing by the day. I could be a librarian anywhere, really, but I love this town and have no desire to live anywhere else.

I just want someone to share my life here with me. For the last six years, that was Sam.

He was a graduation present from my parents when I'd moved into my first apartment. I had three roommates, Hayley, Fiona, and Sam. The other girls loved him as much as I did. He was four years old when my folks picked him up from a Lab rescue group, but he was ready to love and be loved, and so was I.

I park in front of my half of the duplex, my eyes automatically going to the front bay window where Sam would have always been waiting, his eyes on me, and his nose against the window. When he was a few years younger, he would have leaped off the window seat to wait for me by the door, tail wagging ecstatically. More recently, he slid carefully off, if he could get up there at all, thanks to a bad back and arthritic hips. But he'd always beat me to the door.

Tonight, I only see darkness in my window.

The curtains flutter in the matching bay window of the other half of the duplex and ten seconds later, Rose's door opens. Donning a cream faux-fur hat and elegant matching wool car coat that reaches to her shins, Rose picks her way down the five steps to the sidewalk. She's holding the leash of her petite gray schnauzer, Miss Petunia Petalbottom. Clutching Sam's picture, I wait to greet them.

"Oh, Sarah, you're home. How was your day?" Rose's sweet smile bursts off her face from a foot below mine. She's small enough to make Thumbelina feel like an Amazon. And although I know it's not true, she always greets me with "Oh, Sarah" as if she'd been mulling over what a sad sack I am.

"Not bad." I lean down to greet the dog who obliges by putting her front paws on my knees. "Hello, Miss P. Who's a good girl? Who's a very good girl?"

The schnauzer barks sharply and dances on her back feet. There's no doubt that the very good girl is her.

"How was your day, Rose?" I ask.

"I'm awfully busy. This wedding planning will be the death of me, I'm sure. I'm so glad I never had daughters."

"What can I do?" I'd realized soon after we met that telling me she's busy is Rose's way of asking for help.

She takes my arm. "If you have a few minutes, I'd love to show you the sample invitations Charles and I are trying to choose between."

"Of course."

"Thank you, Sarah bird. Come inside where it's warm, and I'll get you a cup of tea."

I take the leash and let Miss P, er, pee on the strip of wheat-brown grass fronting our duplex, while Rose opens her door. She leads me through her front door and hangs her coat on an old-fashioned coat rack instead of the closet. I hang my own coat and Miss P's leash alongside it. The dog runs to her water bowl in the kitchen and drinks.

Rose's half of the duplex couldn't look less like mine. I prefer a modern style with clean walls and surfaces, a lot of gray and white, and a few pops of color.

My friend's home looks like a flower garden crept in and had babies all over the furniture and decor. Everywhere I look, there's a floral pattern of some kind—from the couch to the tablecloth on the table to the pillows on the tiny leather wing-back chairs. And while I try to pick up a bouquet at the grocery store once in a while, she always has at least four arrangements on everything from the kitchen counter to the fireplace mantle. Flower power doesn't begin to describe it.

"Vanilla chamomile?" she asks.

"Yes, please."

Rose seems to have hot water boiling in perpetuity in her electric kettle. It took her months to warm up, so to speak, to the newfangled contraption I'd bought her for Christmas a year ago. She was used to the metal kind you put on the stovetop, but now she loves her new one.

I sit at the dining table where six wedding invitations lay in two careful rows of three. I can tell at a glance that I like pretty much all of them. Or more accurately, I can't tell the difference between them. They're all elegant: cream with black typesetting and nearly indistinguishable fonts.

I call to Miss P, who jumps in my lap and looks at the cards along with me. Rose knows all too well that I'm in dog withdrawal. I've even borrowed Miss P overnight when I've felt especially lonely since Sam died.

I'm tired and hungry, but honestly, I'd rather be here, scratching Miss P's chest and evaluating Rose's sextuplet of identical invitation samples, than at home listening to the clock tick and missing Sam.

My friend putters into the dining room, steaming cups in each hand. She sets one in front of me.

"So, what do you think? I prefer this one." She touches the corner of an invitation announcing the nuptials of two people named Amanda and Saul. "Only, Charles was drawn to this one." She touches another with the names of the happy fake couple, Jin and Dae.

In any other setting, I'd laugh at the idea of a man being "drawn" to a wedding invitation. But Charles has impeccable taste. He owned an antique shop in town for years, and now he lives in the fanciest independent-to-assisted living community in town. He's had an opinion about every decision they've made for their wedding so far, and I admire how he and Rose compromise so well. I'm not sure I'd be able to deal with a man who had to have a say in absolutely everything, but Rose doesn't seem to mind.

"Charles and I both know who's boss," she told me once with a wink. I think she meant herself, but I'm still not sure.

My eyes slide between the two invitations. The only difference I can detect is a slightly fussier font choice in Charles's favorite.

"I like yours," I say.

Rose sighs. "I had a feeling you'd say that. Now I have to convince him."

"How will you do it?" I ask.

She sighs. "Probably make bedroom eyes at him."

I burst out laughing, which startles Miss P. She was settling down in my lap, but she jumps up again. "Bedroom eyes?"

She smiles sweetly. "You should try it the next time you have a serious relationship with a young man."

"Whenever that will be." Ben's face swims in front of my eyes, but I push it away. He'd probably be gone in the Blink of a Lie again.

"Who will you invite to our wedding?" Rose asks. "Surely you won't come alone. You're the maid of honor."

"Maybe I'll ask Ricardo, the security guard at work."

Rose harrumphs like I knew she would. "Oh, not that man. He won't let me park in the open delivery space when I come to drop off my books."

This is not the first time I've heard her complaint. "Rose, no one's supposed to park there. It's for deliveries."

"The space is always empty when I'm there. Why not make it a five minute only space for the book drop?"

"Because then when the delivery van comes, it will sit in the parking lot blocking lots of other spaces."

She waves a hand around, dismissing my comment. "Well. I think he could overlook me taking up the space for a moment."

If he did that, he'd be ignoring it for everyone all day. But her idea of a five-minute drop-off space is a good one. I'll suggest it in our staff meeting for the next time our parking lot is repainted.

I sip my tea. The vanilla flavor is creamy and soothing. "When is the appointment with Le Gateau Gastronomique again?" Rose had invited me to try cake flavors with them. One of the major perks of being the MOH in my book.

"Oh yes, we had to move it due to Charles's cardiology appointment."

Charles has a lot of medical appointments, while Rose, ten years his junior at sixty-five years old, only sees her doctor once a year. Again, this hasn't seemed to bother them. Ever since they met at a charity auction two years ago through Rose's friends Sylvia and Lucia, they've been inseparable. Nothing has kept them apart—not their age difference, health problems (or lack of them), his two ex-wives, or Rose's annoying daughter-in-law, Andrea.

Not even the fact that Rose says she'll keep her place instead of moving in with him. I need my own space sometimes after all these years, she's told me. That was a huge relief. I can't imagine not having Rose next door.

Anyway, it was love at first sight with Charles, Rose told me, and that's all there was to it. If only it were so easy for everyone.

She lets me know the new appointment day and time, and I put it in my phone calendar. Then we drink the rest of our tea and chat about our weeks as Miss P snores daintily in my lap.

When it's finally time to leave, I wish Rose would ask me to sleep in her guest room like she has a few times before when I was a wreck over Sam. Or maybe I can borrow Miss P. I dread going home alone.

Sam, why did you have to leave?

Chapter Six

Ben
Lost Paws, Session Two

Tell us a favorite story about your pet.

Those words are on the whiteboard as I take my seat in the circle. It's funny how we're all back in the seats we started in last week for the first Lost Paws session. Humans are definitely creatures of habit.

Everyone's here except for Sarah. I check my watch. Two minutes until group starts. Bev's chatting with Patricia and Oscar, Lydia seems to be praying silently, and Brent's asleep in the chair next to me. Figures.

Did Sarah quit? Did she decide the group wasn't right for her or that pet grief support was a bunch of crap? I can't say I didn't think the same thing over the last week. But I came back—because of her.

Bev walks to the front of the room. She's wearing the same dog shirt, short pants, and sandals combo again this week. Don't her feet get cold? It still feels like winter out there.

"Welcome back, friends. I'd like to start by reminding you of the rules and asking if you have any thoughts, questions, or comments about last week's group."

Bev runs through the rules again. As she says the one about not fraternizing with other members outside of group, my eyes slide to Sarah's empty chair and then to the door.

Is she coming? If she's not coming, I'll invent an excuse to leave in a few minutes. No reason to stay if she's quit. Bev's face looks expectant; she must have asked us a question.

Lydia raises her hand. "I felt closer to Sister after the last group." She crosses herself. "I could feel her spirit with me as I said my vespers this week."

Bev smiles. "That's wonderful to hear, Lydia. Would anyone else like to share anything about their week?"

I glance at Brent. He's still asleep, so I nudge him awake. He's paying for this, might as well get his money's worth. Although I barely touch him, he shoots out of his chair and shouts a curse word.

We all stare for a second. Lydia recovers first.

"Young man! Your language is offensive to the Lord." She clutches her rosary, her accent thicker.

"Are you all right, Brent?" Bev asks cautiously.

He runs a hand through his thick brown hair and sits. "Yeah, I'm okay. I haven't been sleeping well." He mutters something about bad dreams.

I lean over to him. "Sorry I startled you."

He nods but doesn't say anything, thrusting his hands into the large pocket of his hoodie. It's an old Denver Nuggets sweatshirt that has pieces of some kind of dry grass sticking to it.

Bev clears her throat and asks again if anyone has something to say.

"I have a question," Patricia says. "Is it common to think more about your pet, and maybe miss them more, after the first week of group?" She asks the question casually, but her eyes sport dark smudges underneath.

Bev nods sagely. "You may find that you spend more time thinking or even dreaming about your pet these first few weeks. You could feel more anxious or sad. This is all normal."

"How about more hungry?" Oscar asks. "I had two plates of *barbacoa* last night, but my stomach still growled. Edith says she's tired of cooking for three—her, me, and my second stomach." He laughs.

Bev starts to answer, but she's interrupted as Sarah rushes into the room. Something in my gut unclenches as she sits across from me, pink-cheeked and whispering apologies to everyone.

"Welcome, Sarah," Bev says. "We've been talking about how we're doing after last week. Patricia has been thinking about Snickerdoodle more, and Oscar said he's been hungrier."

Sarah puts her bag down and nods sympathetically at them. I try to catch her eye, but she doesn't look my way.

"I wish I could eat," Brent says. "I went to McDonald's yesterday and walked straight back out. Nothing sounded good, and it smelled like crap in there."

Patricia grunts. "If only. I'm like Oscar. I can't seem to push away from the table, and if there's Ben and Jerry's in the freezer?" She shakes her head. "Uh-uh. That pint is history by bedtime."

Sarah laughs. "I avoid the freezer aisles these days. If I so much as walk past the frozen desserts, I can't be responsible for my behavior."

Patricia gives her a knowing look. "Tell me about it."

Bev jumps in. "One thing to learn about major losses is that we won't experience life the same way after. You've all lost a VIB —Very Important Being. We need to be patient and kind with ourselves as we adjust to life without them." She walks to the whiteboard. "Now, I suspect that it was hard for some of you to talk about your pets last week. Others, I would guess, might have wanted to tell us more about them."

She points to the sentence. "Today's exercise is for the

second group. I'd like to ask you to tell a favorite story about your pet."

Lydia's hand goes up, but Brent speaks first. "Do we have to?"

Bev shakes her head vigorously. "I'll never force you to do anything you aren't comfortable with in this space. I only ask that you listen to your peers respectfully."

Brent nods and shoves his hands back in his hoodie pocket. I catch a whiff of weed off him every time he moves. Bev calls on Lydia.

"I'd like to tell the story of how Sister Mary Margaret came to me," Lydia says. And there's the sign of the cross.

"Excellent," Bev says. "Please do."

Lydia settles herself in her chair. "It was ten years ago, when my Brother was still alive." She laughs. "He would sit beside me and lick my hand every now and again to remind me he was there."

I glance around. We all looked grossed out.

"Your . . . brother . . . licked your hand?" Bev asks carefully.

Lydia nods. "Yes, right before he curled up and went to sleep on his mat. Where he was often flatulent." She titters. "My Brother Brendan Kevin was named for two Irish saints. One who explored the world, searching for the Garden of Eden, and one who sat still so long, birds nested in his hands."

Bev is red in the face, but suddenly her eyes open wide. "Oh! Brother was a dog."

Lydia looks puzzled. "Yes, of course. What else?"

Sarah's hiding a smile behind her hand. I'm having a hard time not cracking up.

Lydia shakes her head and goes on. "One day, a friend who breeds Saint Bernards brought her female with her for a visit. While we were having our tea and a catch up, the dogs played in the garden. She left, and Brother and I went about our evening. Well, a few weeks later, my friend rings me up and tells me her female is pregnant, and Brother is the father." Her lips pucker as she fingers her rosary.

"You can imagine my shock. Brother was old by then, well past his prime. What they got up to back there, I can only imagine."

Um, I can imagine. And it's a funny mental picture. Saint Bernards are massive.

Lydia goes on. "Six weeks later, my friend rings again, and asks if I'd like to come 'round to see Brother's puppies. Well, I did, and I took one home, too. Later that year, my Brother passed, but I had the comfort of Sister Mary Margaret. The pregnancy was God's will."

Lydia paws through her bag. "Would you all like to see a picture of Sister when she was a pup? She was the most darling thing."

She shows the photo to Sarah, who breaks into a smile, then she passes it to Patricia and Oscar, who make appreciative noises. I can't help grinning when it comes to me. Sister was a white and brown fluff ball with black coal chips for eyes. I pass it to Brent, who barely looks at it before giving it to Bev. Bev admires it and hands it back to Lydia.

Lydia touches her handkerchief to her nose and tucks the photo back in her bag. "Out of sin comes divine innocence."

I scratch my head. It's a sin when dogs mate?

Oscar speaks up. "My favorite story about Baloney is the time he caught some *cholo* trying to steal from our apartment." He rubs his jaw stubble. "Edith and I were at work, and Baloney and Cheese were probably asleep in the closet. They liked our closet for some reason. So, a man broke in through the back door—I had to replace the door after the ass—," he glances at Lydia apologetically, "the dude split the wood around the lock forcing his way in. Anyway, he must have woke up the cats because some neighbors saw him running down the back alley, his face all scratched up. The cops picked him up the next day—because of Baloney's scratch marks."

"Was Baloney okay?" Patricia asks.

"When we got home, he was perched on the kitchen counter,

watching the back door like the guy might come back." Oscar beams at the memory, his eyes a little wet, and then shakes his head. "He was a really good cat."

I can't argue with that. Who wouldn't want an attack cat guarding their house?

"Thank you for sharing, Oscar. Who's next?" Bev asks.

No one volunteers. Sarah glances my way, as if seeing if I might raise my hand. I'm not planning on it. I don't want to make my lie worse by telling an ancient Bailey story. But then, Sarah speaks to me.

"What about you, Ben?" She says it like a challenge.

Bev clucks her tongue. "Ben doesn't need to share if he's not comfortable."

"No, it's okay." If Sarah wants a story, I'll give her one. "My favorite Bailey story is the day he got out of the house. It was late, and we didn't realize he was gone until the next morning. We freaked out, and my mom sent me down to the neighbor's houses to look for him."

Sarah's forehead wrinkles. "Your . . . mom?"

I clench my teeth. Whoops. "She was, uh, visiting that week. Anyway, I showed Bailey's picture all over the neighborhood, but no one had seen him. Like an hour and a half later, a lady opened the door and recognized him right away. She let me in, and right there in her kitchen was Bailey, sitting on a barstool eating a full sausage and egg breakfast out of a pasta bowl. Turns out, he had wandered onto her porch late the night before, and she took him in. Her husband had died a few months before, she said, and she was lonely. She figured he'd sent Bailey to her that night to keep her company. She said the least she could do was feed him a good breakfast."

Sarah's eyes glitter a little with tears. Bull's-eye. The Bailey story is true, by the way. Every word. Except for my mom visiting and all. She lived there. And I still played Legos and dressed up like a Ghostbuster for Halloween.

Bev thanks me for sharing and moves on to Patricia and her

story of how Snickerpoodle saved a kid from being hit by a car, but I feel Sarah's eyes on me a few seconds longer than anyone else's.

Which gives me hope. Maybe this inane plan of mine to get to know Sarah again will work. Or . . . maybe she'll find out I'm a lying sack of dog poo.

Either way, the suspense is killing me. And it's my own damn fault.

Chapter Seven

Sarah

Ben's story about Bailey gets to me.

Sam got out of the house once, and for the three hours he was missing, I'd thought I would lose my mind. The image of Bailey eating breakfast off a plate hit pretty close to home, too. Don't judge; I'd run the dishwasher on super-hot to disinfect.

As the others tell their own stories, I try to come up with my favorite one about Sam. There was the time after I first got him when he'd happily chewed the plastic heads off of the holy family in the nativity set that my grandmother had given me. I was horrified, but it was also kind of funny. My roommates joked he was going straight to hell.

Or the time Sam snuck to the kitchen and ate an entire large pepperoni pizza, threw it up on my bed in the middle of the night, and was in the process of enjoying it again when I'd woken up. Or the time I'd come home after work one Halloween to find a whole mega bag of chocolate candy had been carefully unwrapped and eaten, resulting in piles of poop all over the house. Trick or treat!

In the end, I tell the pizza one. Some of the best pet tales are when they do something dreadful in the moment but humorous to tell after the fact.

Honestly, the most memorable thing about Sam was how he'd made me feel. Warm, loved, and safe. And hopefully, I'd made him feel the same. It just didn't make for a very good yarn.

I have to run to the restroom at the end of group, and then I spend an extra five minutes buttoning the vintage wool coat that I thought was so cute when I'd bought it because of the dozen decorative buttons up the front. (Mistake, for the record.) And I fuss over arranging my scarf in the mirror. Which means I'm behind everyone else as I leave the church.

Some of the lights around the rear parking lot are burned out, and the ones that are lit are dim. As I hurry toward my car in the parking lot, someone grabs my arm from the shadows.

I scream . . . but not fearfully. More, um, aggressive than that. I add a side kick to my attacker's torso followed by a jab to his chin with my left fist.

Luckily, the jab doesn't connect. The guy's already heading toward the ground; I took him out with the kick.

I lean over to get a look at my attacker. Oops. It's Ben.

He's on his butt, legs tented, head between his knees, breathing hard. I squat next to him, and my giant tote bag rams him in the side of the head on the way down.

"Oh my gosh, I'm so sorry," I say. "You grabbed my arm, and . . . I'm so sorry!" I touch his arm. "Are you okay?"

"Yes . . . only . . . humiliated," he says. "Where did you learn to kick like that?"

"The Kickbutt Kickboxing channel on YouTube. It's what I do for exercise."

He winces and rubs his stomach. "They should give you a black belt."

"Can I get you anything?" I ask. "Some water?"

"Yeah, and an unbruised ego on the side."

I smile. "I am really sorry."

"How about a hand up, instead?"

"Of course." I take his hand and lift, but I pull too hard and yank him right into me so we're smashed chest to chest.

Awkward. But my heart trips over itself to have him so close. We'd only gone so far as kissing back in the day, but bodies don't forget this stuff. I brush dirt off the arm of his coat and step away.

A hand on his chest, he breathes a full breath.

"Are you sure there's not anything I can do?" Apparently, I can be obnoxiously obsequious after assaulting people.

He pauses. "Actually, since you asked . . . would you have coffee with me?"

I blink. That was the last thing I thought he'd say.

I literally feel myself shrink. "I don't know."

He makes a face. "Come on, it's the least you can do after kicking my butt."

"You shouldn't have grabbed me like that!"

"Clearly," he laughs. "I'll keep that in mind moving forward, too." He peeks at me from under his lashes and smiles. I'd forgotten he did that. It's so . . . beguiling. "So, coffee?"

I should say no. I really should. After all, he was dishonest years ago Without Batting a Lie. But it's only coffee. I'm not agreeing to marry him or anything. And he does seem different now. More mature, I guess.

I sigh. Let's face it, it's been a long time since someone born after 1965 showed an interest in me.

"Sure," I say, but then I remember. "Wait—it's against the group rules."

He winks. "I won't tell Bev if you don't. Where do you want to go?"

I think for a second. There's only one really good café close by.

"Alleycat?" I suggest reluctantly. "We can walk from here."

He meets my eyes—remembering our first date, too, I assume—and smiles. My heart quivers. What am I doing going for coffee again with Ben Becker?

As we set off in the direction of College Avenue, I notice him absentmindedly rub his abdomen again.

"Are you sure you're all right?" I ask.

"I am. Really. Except I'm sorry I startled you." He pauses. "Honestly, I probably deserved it."

He says this without a soupçon of humor, so I don't really know how to respond. Was that . . . an apology?

Overhead, the stars twinkle in the clear sky. I think about bringing up the weather, that tired conversational standby, but I don't want to come across as prosaic right off the bat.

"Your Bailey story was really sweet," I say instead.

"Thanks."

He winces as if the memory is painful, which is . . . also really sweet. Then he hurries on.

"That pizza story was hilarious."

I adjust my bag. "I couldn't pick one! I have so many favorites, and I spent the whole time arguing with myself about which one to tell until we nearly ran out of time." The barely scabbed-over wound in my heart pricks open again. "On second thought, can we not talk about our dogs?"

"Got it. Dogs are off limits. How about our jobs? Are they safe?"

I laugh. "Mine is. Libraries are definitely my safe space."

He snorts. "Does that make my cubicle my safe space? Because that's incredibly depressing, actually."

I laugh. "I just love my job and my library. They make me happy."

Along with Ang and Rose, they're two of the few things that do these days, I don't say. Ben's already seen me crying pitifully two or three times. I'm determined to prove I'm an adult with full emotional control now.

Most of the time.

"That's so cool that you found your passion in college," he says.

I glance at a van rolling by. When I look over, the shadowy driver speeds up and carries on down the road.

"Didn't you?" I ask Ben.

He shrugs. Since we're walking side by side, I feel it more than see it as the arm of his coat slides by mine. "I wouldn't call software engineering a passion. I like it, I make good money. It's okay for now."

We turn right onto College and head halfway down the block to Alleycat. The coffee shop is on the second floor of the building, over DGT Tacos and Algiers Hookah and Shisha.

"I haven't been here in a while," I say as we climb the stairs.

"Doesn't look like it's changed much."

Caffeine addicts from yuppies to hipsters sit at the wood tables around the cafe. Painted squares in different artistic styles line the ceiling above their heads. A long bar holds the register, empty mugs and glasses waiting to be filled, and a couple of plants. Art pieces featuring all kinds of cats lounge around the space, and of course, the warm, toasty scent of coffee fills my nose.

"Why don't you grab a table, and I'll get drinks. What would you like?" Ben asks.

I scan the menu. "How about a Honey Buzz Latte?" Vanilla, cinnamon, and honey could never, ever be bad.

"You got it."

I find a table in the corner by the window and leave my coat and scarf on for now. I'm still chilled from the walk here. I check my phone in case Angela, Rose, or my family called. Nothing. It's an hour ahead in Omaha, so almost my parents' bedtime. Rose will be nodding off soon in front of *Midsomer Murders*, one of her favorite British cozy mystery series. She's gotten me into them, too. I'm only on season ten, but she doesn't mind rewatching episodes.

A man waves from across the cafe. It's Franklin, a patron at the library, one of my favorites. He has a physical disability that causes him to walk unsteadily and to be unable to use his left arm. I think it might prevent him from working, because he's at the library for hours most days. When I wave back, he holds up his library book, something sci-fi from the spaceship cruising across the cover. I give him a thumbs-up.

Ben glances at Franklin as he sets our drinks down. "A friend?"

"A library patron, and a nice guy."

Franklin waves at Ben, too, and Ben waves back. I think about suggesting that we invite him over, but frankly, I'm too selfish. This is feeling more and more like a date, and I haven't exactly had scads of those lately. Even if it is with Mr. Frequent Liar.

"Do you see many friends from CSU anymore?" Ben asks.

"A few sorority sisters. We get together once a month for drinks and dinner or to see a movie. Mostly, I spend time with my friend, Angela, and my neighbor, Rose."

I tell him a little about them.

"So, you'll be in both of their weddings soon?" He whistles. "Double duty."

I roll my eyes. "I feel like it's been my summer job the last five years. This will be my seventh and eighth weddings since college."

"Popular girl."

Ha. Not exactly. But I do seem to be a popular choice for bridesmaid. He wipes his mouth with his napkin. He's drinking black coffee, which makes me feel comparatively silly with my pint glass of sugary confection topped with a mound of sweet foam. On the other hand, it's absolutely scrummy. I'm tempted to lick the glass clean when it's gone.

"Don't get me wrong," I say, "I love my friends, but being the maid of honor means dress shopping, planning the bachelorette party or the bachelorette weekend, running interference with difficult relatives at the wedding . . . you name it, I do it. Oh, and I'm the CMO."

He squints. "What's that?"

"Chief Meltdown Officer. One of my friends dubbed me that a few years ago."

Ben smiles, and I remember he has dimples. Dimples! Can he be any cuter? That's enough, Sarah. He's an ugly, ugly lying man. With adorable dimples.

"You're the wedding wingman," he says.

"Wing*woman.*"

He grins. "So . . . is there a wingman to your wingwoman role?"

I hesitate. I got a little lost. Is he asking about the best men? "I, well—I'm not sure. There are the groomsmen . . ."

He blushes. Blushing and dimples! My insides melt. "I'm asking—badly—if you have a boyfriend to go with you to all these weddings."

"Oh! No. I mean, not right now."

And yes, since you asked, I'm dreading going to my friends' weddings without a date. But why is he asking? Is he interested? Wait, I'm not interested. Really.

A man slides into the booth next to me. I yelp, and my arm flies up, elbow at the ready. If he comes any closer, he gets a fat lip. When I see who it is, my arm and jaw drop.

What is Brent doing here?

Chapter Eight

Ben

"I thought that was you guys. Scoot over," Brent says.

Sarah looked frightened for a second, but now she seems confused.

"Hey, Brent. Uh, how'd you know we were here?" I ask.

"I was driving out of the church parking lot, and I saw you guys walking together. I circled the block and followed you here."

Sarah's eyes go wide. "Do you drive a van?"

He nods. "I thought we weren't supposed to, like, fraternize with each other." He holds up a hand to her and then to me to high-five. "Right on, rebels. I like rule breakers. Hey, can I bum a few bucks for a coffee?"

"Sure. I . . . guess." With an apologetic look at Sarah, I dig in my wallet.

Brent glances at the cash there. "Those blueberry muffins looked pretty good, too."

I tug out two more dollars and hand them over.

"Be right back." He heads for the register.

Sarah and I exchange bewildered looks.

"What should we do?" she whispers.

I shake my head and laugh ruefully. "Get to know Brent better, I guess."

Fantastic. Brent crashed my sort-of date with Sarah. Not to mention, he probably thinks Sarah is as awesome as I do. He definitely checks her out in group when she's not looking—and even when she is looking—which makes me want to punch him a few times. Not hard. Only enough to knock him out.

He sits back down with the coffee and muffin I bought him and looks from Sarah to me.

"So, what's up? What's with the extra group sesh?"

I clear my throat. "Uh, nothing really. We didn't have an agenda or anything. We just didn't feel like going home yet."

He slurps from his mug and takes a huge bite of the baked good—paper lining and all. We stare at him like he's popped a cockroach in his mouth.

"What?" he says. "It's compostable."

Sarah snorts with laughter, but I think he's lost it.

"So, what do you guys think of the group?" Brent asks through a mouthful of crumbles.

She answers. "It's good. I like it. I don't know if it's helping yet or anything, but it feels better to be with other people who really understand what I'm feeling."

And . . . cue the guilt. I squirm in my seat, making Brent look over. I scratch my back against the back of the chair as cover.

"That Bev is a trip, though, right? The shirt cracks me up." Brent grunts as he takes another giant swallow of coffee. The guy must have a throat of iron with the way he can guzzle a hot beverage like that.

"I like her." Sarah sounds a little defensive. "I think she really understands what it's like for us."

"I've had worse therapists," Brent says. "Lots of 'em."

Sarah's surprised gaze slides to me, then back to Brent.

"What about you, Brent? Do you like the group?" I ask.

From what I know about group dynamics, the make up of the people is pretty important. One person can scuttle the whole thing. And of all of us, Brent seems the least likely to fit in.

"Doesn't really matter what I think. I have to be there. My PO is making me."

"PO?" Sarah asks.

He wipes his mouth with the back of his hand. "Parole officer."

Sarah's eyebrows shoot into her hairline this time. I almost choke on my coffee.

"Oh." Sarah licks her lips. "Um, what did you, you know, do? If you don't mind me asking."

"Grand theft."

She looks fascinated.

I shift in my seat. "What did you steal?"

"Rats. From Patrick's Perfect Pets down on Olive Street."

"Rats?" I repeat. "Like . . . rodents?"

He snorts. "What other kind are there?"

"Are they . . . the ones in your freezer?" Sarah says.

"Yep, those."

"*Why?*" I ask.

Brent shoots me what can only be described as a withering look. "Because Sev was hungry, and I couldn't afford to pay for them."

I nod. Not a great excuse, but point taken.

"How much time did you get for stealing frozen rats?" Sarah asks.

Brent leans back and stretches an arm across the seat back behind her. If he touches her, I'm dragging him out of here. After she knocks him out with a roundhouse, that is.

"Nine months," Brent says.

"For rats?" Sarah asks.

"It was a lot of rats. And some money." He snorts, probably in response to our horrified expressions. "No one was hurt or anything. And it was all for Sev. Seriously. I wasn't going to let him go hungry. Been there, done that myself. It sucks."

Sarah and I nod dutifully. I can't say for sure about her, but I doubt either of us has ever gone hungry unless we were on a diet. And I've never really tried to lose weight, so I can't even say I've done that.

"What do you do for work, Brent?" I ask.

He looks around the coffee shop and yawns as if he's already bored with us. "I work at a pet store."

"What? They hired you, after . . . you know?" Sarah asks.

"Sure. They know what I did. But they didn't need to know where I stole from. Now, I get a discount on stuff from the store, so if I get another snake, I can afford to feed him. Then again, I've never kept a job for longer than a few months."

Sarah studies him. "What would you do? Like, if you could do anything?"

He rubs his face. "Hell, I don't know. I don't even know what I'll eat for breakfast tomorrow."

Well, I know what he ate for dinner. Coffee and a muffin on me.

Sarah's eyes sparkle. "I saw that look on your face, though. You have an idea."

Brent lays the tines of his fork on the end of the table and slaps down on it, it flies in the air, and he catches it. "It's nothing. Stupid idea that I can't afford to do anyway."

"What?" she asks. "Tell us. Better yet, tell the universe. It's more likely to happen that way."

Brent stares at her. "What a bunch of—Okay." He jumps up onto the booth seat. "Attention, everyone, attention."

The café customers quiet down in that nervous, watchful way people do when someone acts odd. Sarah and I stare at Brent, mouths open.

"I want to be a veterinary technician. Maybe even an actual veterinarian one day." He pauses. "That is all."

He flops back down on the seat beside Sarah. "That good enough for the universe?"

"That was great, Brent." Sarah touches his shoulder. "And brave."

He shrugs and slams the end of the fork again. "Not that it will change anything. The universe only changes for rich people."

"It's the money stopping you?" I ask.

"Isn't it stopping everyone?"

Another good point. "Student loans?"

"Yeah, I guess I could apply for those. I don't know, bro, I like animals and thought helping them instead of selling them might be cool. At the rate I'm going, though, I'll be eligible for a prestigious position in either the Animal Control or Solid Waste Services after my current opportunity ends."

Sarah pats the table excitedly. "Brent! I have an amazing vet you could talk to. His name is Travis Brewer, and he and his fiancée Amelia, who's also his tech, run a mobile vet practice called Love & Pets. They were so wonderful with Sam the last few years. Do you want to talk to them? I can call him and ask if he has time."

Brent hunches over. "Yeah, sure. Sometime."

Sarah lays her hand on his arm, which makes my jaw involuntarily clench. "Not sometime. Now. The universe is waiting. I dare you. Wait, you don't have to stand on the seat and announce it though!"

His eyes narrow. I don't get the sense this guy has backed down from too many dares in his life.

"Fine. Call him."

Sarah turns to me, her smile dazzling. "We're witnesses, Ben. Right?"

I nod and grin myself. Her excitement is charming, even if it's directed at Brent. "Right."

"I'll call Travis and let you know what he says by next group," she tells Brent.

He nudges her shoulder with his. "Thanks."

Okay, there's entirely too much touching going on between them. It can stop any time now. And then they smile at each other. Hers is bright and sunny and his cloudier, but they're both genuine.

I feel like I'm intruding on their special moment.

Wait, what happened here? Is Sarah into snake-loving, tattooed, parolee Brent?

Chapter Nine

Sarah

"Hey, you two, I'm sorry I'm late."

I slip into the back room of Le Gateau Gastronomique after being directed there by a bored French guy at the bakery counter. Rose and Charles are already seated.

Rose pats the seat next to her. "It's all right, Sarah bird. They're about to bring out our first option." She gestures to the kitchen beyond, of which I can only see a sliver through a swinging door.

Mmm, sliver. We're trying the cake flavors today.

I hug Rose and reach around her to squeeze Charles's hand. He's wearing a dark suit and complementary shirt and tie, as usual, complete with a pocket square. His hair is a pretty silver, which stands out against his exceptionally tanned skin. I asked Rose once if he used a tanning bed to stay that dark year-round, but she only winked at me in response.

"How's your back?" I ask him.

"I shouldn't complain," he says with his clipped accent, "but I will. It's agony. I feel like someone's driving an antique nail into my lower spine and tapping it every so often with a hammer."

Rose frowns and squeezes her fiancé's arm. Charles's accent has always interested me. It's not quite American, not quite British, maybe European? When he's asked, he always answers, I'm a man of the world. So, maybe Canada.

"Why an antique nail?" I say.

He looks down his nose at me. I don't take offense. He looks down his nose at everyone. It's a side-effect of being a graduate of Oxford University and a successful businessman. Rose said she knew he loved her when he stopped looking down his nose at her and "looked at me square."

"There is nothing modern on this body," he answers. "Thank God."

A woman clicks into the room carrying a tray. She wears high heels, a pencil skirt, and a silk blouse complemented by a scarf. She's middle aged, but she covers it well with expertly applied makeup.

As she sets the tray on the table in front of us, I admire her ability to walk confidently in those shoes. You don't see heels of that teetering height in Fort Collins, Colorado very often.

Expecting an elegant French accent that matches her appearance, I wait for her to introduce the slim slices of cake on the tray.

"Ah, our mad adorner shrive," she says. "*Bon jour*, jam a Nicorette, prostitute of Le Gateau."

Or at least that's what it sounds like. She's speaking some kind of Franglish . . . I think. I look to Rose and Charles for help, but they don't seem fazed. I guess they're used to—Nicorette's—way of speaking.

"Hi, I'm Sarah." Prostitute of the Old Town Library doesn't have quite the same ring to it.

The woman puts a manicured hand on her hip and gestures at the tray. "Set the *vanille*. Sample class eggplant. Views ally adorable."

I have no idea what the *vanille* she's saying, but my mouth waters at the sight of the light and airy cake slices on creamy china plates. They look absolutely delectable, and the smell . . . vanilla with a hint of cinnamon? Divine.

Nicorette distributes a plate to each of us with a delicate silver fork. I could easily scoop that sucker up and shove it in with one behemoth bite, but instead, I wait for Rose and Charles to try theirs, and then cut a reasonable chunk.

The sweet yet light flavor comes through cleanly from my sample. A groan nearly slips out. I manage to hold myself back from gobbling another forkful for long enough to say, "Delicious."

"It is. *Magnifique*, Nicolette," Rose says.

Oh, so she's not named for a smoking cessation aid.

Charles doesn't speak until his piece is gone. He touches his mouth with a napkin and nods his approval. Personally, I have trouble not licking my finger to pick up the last crumbs from the plate.

Next up is chocolate ganache for the groom's cake, and it's equally luscious. As Nicolette retreats into the kitchen to fetch something that sounds like *seat tron a la con feature from Boise*, whatever that might be, I consider sneaking in behind her and kidnapping the nearest freshly baked wedding cake in sight.

Then I remember: I have to fit into my MOH dresses. Rose already told me that other than the color—pale dove-gray—I can choose my own dress, so I did, but Ang wants me to wear a tight-fitting number in pale pink.

After Nicolette brings out the cake slices—a sublime lemon cake with raspberry filling—she offers us a last sample of an unusual rose flavored blush-tinted cake frosted with vanilla.

Each sample is better than the last. We finish our plates leaving nary a morsel.

"Well," Rose asks Charles and me, "what do you two think?"

"The lemon," I say. "Classic but still inspired."

Charles agrees. "It was *fantastique*."

"That settles it." Rose fluffs her hair and stands to speak to Nicolette.

Charles sits back gingerly in his chair. "What are you reading this week?"

We share a love for books, although not all genres. He has a weakness for military history—boring!—and I like contemporary romances, which he loves to tease me about. Thinking of Charles checking out my current read—a seaside romance pairing a lonely fisherman and a young, skittish widow—makes me grin.

"I finished a wonderful historical fiction set in Brazil the other day," I say. "Oh! And I have the book you put on hold."

I fish it out of my tote bag. *Proud Destiny*, the true story of some battalion or another in World War I. Looks like a real snore-fest.

"Excellent. Just in time. I finished the latest Patterson mystery last night. I'll give it to Rose for you."

"Thanks!"

Our one shared guilty pleasure: easy reading, plot-driven mysteries. Reading James Patterson is like sipping an inexpensive chardonnay on the front porch in summer. A pleasant distraction, and before you know it, you look down, and the glass is empty. Time to refill.

Rose returns. "All set. And we have an appointment to finalize the design."

Charles stands a little at a time. "Well, I need to toddle off home for my nap." He naps for an hour every day at three o'clock in the afternoon. He's done it for years, even when he worked. He credits his lack of hair loss and smooth skin to the habit.

I hug him carefully, Rose kisses him goodbye, and then she takes my arm. "Walk me to my car?" We head for the lot, nodding at the counter guy on the way out. "You got in late last night."

For the first few years of living next to Rose, I thought it was odd that she kept tabs on me. Now, trust me, it's comforting. If she didn't keep an eye out, no one would even know if I was eaten by wild dogs like Bridget Jones.

I hesitate. I haven't told Ang, my sister, Liz, or anyone else about my sort of date with Ben after group. My family doesn't even know I'm in a pet grief support group. Not that they wouldn't understand, but I don't want them to worry about me. They live too far away to do anything to help, anyway, other than check on me, which they already do.

Taking a few extra seconds to savor the secret like a toothsome square of expensive dark chocolate, I finally tell Rose about my evening.

She beams. "I wondered if you'd made a new friend in that group!"

She calls it "that group." As if an emotional support group is slightly suspicious.

I shake my head, still a little amazed myself. "Two, actually." I tell her about Brent.

"Well, now. That's strange. Are you sure he's altogether safe?"

"No . . . but, I don't think he's dangerous either. Maybe a little unpredictable? Anyway, it was a fun evening. But I don't think it can happen again." I tell her about the rules.

Rose waves her hand. "Oh, rules schmules. If you like this young man—Ben, not the boy who's been to prison—then see him. What is that woman going to do? Send the therapy police after you?"

I grin. "Rose, I had no idea you were such an anarchist."

She straightens her spine. "You don't get to be my age without understanding that some rules should be broken." Her voice grows serious. "And, Sarah bird, you've been in how many weddings now without a date? You deserve a man on your pretty arm as much or more than anyone. Your sorrow over Sam took up so much of your time in the last year. Let this year be one of joy."

I let her words sink in. Could I pursue things with Ben? Is that even a good idea? Probably not, given our history.

But the idea that I could have a real, live date to this year's weddings instead of going it alone is intoxicating.

I've struggled so much since Sam got sick, I don't remember the last time I wasn't sad. But is Ben the answer?

Chapter Ten

Ben
Lost Paws, Session Three

I get to group early, hoping to catch Sarah and ask if she'd like to get dinner after group this time instead of coffee. And definitely without Brent.

But I find the two of them in deep discussion when I arrive. I flop in my chair and check out the whiteboard.

Tell us about a time you dealt with a difficult emotion like sadness, anger, or bitterness. What did you do? What was the outcome?

Does jealousy count, Bev? How about right now? I glance again at Sarah. She's smiling and moving her hands around like she's really into whatever they're talking about. What could be so exciting? It's *Brent*.

Get a grip, Ben. Sarah's a kind person who's being a lot nicer than you are to a guy down on his luck.

I think about going over and joining in with them, but Bev looks like she's getting ready to get started. I sneak another peek at Sarah. She looks great today in a sweater and skirt combo that hug her curves.

What's my obsession with this woman, anyway? Sarah is sweet, kind, and pretty. But I can name several women at work or in my friend group that could be described that way. What is it about *her*?

I've thought about that over the last two weeks. A lot. I guess it's that, even though we're here for a grief group and everything, and I know she's been really missing Sam, there's something refreshing about her. There's a light that shines from somewhere inside her that draws me right in.

And there's something else. It's bothered me more than I'd like to admit that she thought I lied about Alexa. I had already broken things off with my ex. I'd told her not to call, text, or drop by anymore. But she had suspected I was seeing someone else, so she sent random texts—only in the evenings—probably in hopes that the woman would see them. And damn if it didn't happen.

Even though we'd only gone out a few times, I'd liked Sarah a lot back then. And I still do. I want another chance to prove myself to her.

If only I can keep the fact that I'm completely lying about Bailey from her.

Brent grunts my way as he sits in his chair beside me. Bev hasn't quite finished chatting up Patricia, so I grab my chance and slide into the chair Brent vacated next to Sarah. I keep my voice low.

"Hey, I was wondering if you'd want to grab something to eat after group tonight."

"Oh . . ." Sarah bites her lip, which is way more distracting than it really should be. "I told Brent I'd meet him for coffee again at Alleycat after group. I called my vet, Travis, and Travis called him to set up a meeting. I can tell Brent's excited. Although, you know, he tries to pretend he doesn't care."

I run a hand through my hair, trying to contain my annoyance. "Got it. Well, you guys have a good time."

Sarah touches my arm. "Why don't you come, too? It was fun last week."

"No, that's okay. I don't want to be a third wheel." I get ready to stand; Bev's taking her seat.

Sarah touches my hand and whispers as the group quiets down. "You really are welcome to join us, Ben. I don't think Brent will mind."

I glance at Brent. He's scratching hard at something on his palm, looking very not interested in us. I flash a smile at Sarah and nod. Bev catches my smile, so I flatten my expression and keep my eyes on the group leader.

Bev's eyes narrow a bit, but she moves on. Sock watch, week three: no socks under her sandals this week. Hmm, curious.

"How is everyone? Would anyone like to share?"

Oscar raises his hand. "Edith got a new cat. Her name is Mustard."

He doesn't look happy about it. And what is with the sandwich filling names?

"Did she talk to you about it first?" Patricia says.

"No, Mustard showed up on the back porch, begging for food. Edith fed her a few times, and now *los nietos*, the grandkids, love her, so we can't put her back outside."

"And how do you feel about Mustard?" Bev asks.

Oscar screws up one side of his face. "I don't know. I haven't had much to do with her yet." He thinks about it. "I still miss Baloney. Even Cheese can't take his place."

Bev nods. "That's very normal, Oscar. It might take you more time to have loving feelings for Mustard, or even for Cheese, for that matter. I mean, imagine a spouse dying." Lydia crosses herself. "You wouldn't grab the first man or woman you see on the street who looks a little like them and decide you love them equally as much, would you?"

"I don't know," Lydia says. "My grandmother might have."

We all laugh.

"She never said this outright, but I would be willing to wager she couldn't wait to see the coffin shut on my grandfather. They had a quiet war their whole marriage." Lydia shakes her head. "As an example, he hated peas. And my grandmother knew it full well. So, she made him peas every Sunday after church. Meanwhile, my grandfather knew my grandmother hated the smell of pine. It reminded her of cleaning floors, which she'd done for fifty years. So, when my grandfather would clean the car and buy a new air freshener, he always bought the ones that smelled of pine trees."

Bev makes her therapy face. "Marriage can be quite a challenge."

Brent rubs his stomach. "Baloney, cheese, mustard, peas. This is making me hungry."

I have to agree with him.

Sarah raises her hand. "I've been feeling a little better this week. I'm still sad, and I think about Sam all the time, especially when I'm at home, but it's . . . better." Her eyes shoot to me, then away.

My pulse picks up. Was she telling me she had a better week because of our coffee date? Or am I imagining things? I decide to risk it.

"I'm feeling better, too. I didn't think about Bailey so much this week."

She smiles right at me.

"I ate more this week," Brent says. "If you count doughnuts."

"That's wonderful, Sarah and Ben," Bev says. "And Brent, your appetite coming back could be a sign that you're doing some emotional healing." She stands and walks to the whiteboard. "Speaking of emotions, would anyone like to share about a time when they dealt with a difficult emotion, like I wrote here. How did you feel? What did you do about it? What was the result?"

Patricia raises her hand. Her hair isn't perfectly styled like it was the first two weeks, I notice, and she's wearing a sweat suit instead of her usual sharp pantsuit. "Honestly, I'm dealing with a difficult emotion right now. I want to divorce my husband."

Bev's therapist face is in full force now. "I'm so sorry, Patricia. Tell us about it."

"I had an argument with Raymond this week about Snicker-doodle. He told me he's never liked her and that he doesn't want another dog, or any kind of pet, after her." She throws an angry hand in the air. "And he's telling me this now? We've been married for five years, and I've had Snickers that whole time. When was he going to mention that he hated my dog and didn't like pets? Who does that?"

Lydia shakes her head sharply. "Stay far away from men who don't love animals. They might be serial killers. Mass murderers. Rapists. Or worse, atheists."

Brent and I snicker. Bev's staring at Lydia, mouth open.

"Yes, well, I'm not sure all that is true," she turns back to Patricia, "but it is a concern that he kept this from you. How did he treat Snickerdoodle when she was alive?"

Patricia huffs. "I mean, he wasn't cruel to her or anything, but he also didn't pay much attention to her. That's part of what's bothering me—how did I not notice he didn't like her? Did I miss something else? Could Ray have been kicking her behind my back or shoving her off the couch when I went to the bathroom? Is he even who I thought he was?"

I speak up. "Have you asked him why he didn't tell you?"

Patricia makes a face. "He said he wasn't sure how to tell me. But he should have been straight with me about how he felt. What's next? He doesn't like children?"

Patricia looks fiftyish—maybe too old to have kids, I think. But what do I know?

"Have you all discussed having children?" Bev asks gently.

Patricia quirks her eyebrow. "At my age? You've got to be kidding. My babies are grown up and out of the house. I'm waiting to be a grandma any day now . . . but that's what I'm worried about. When we have grandbabies, will Raymond suddenly decide he doesn't like them either?"

"How did you leave things with him?" Bev asks.

"I told him I needed a break. I'm not sure I can truly love a man who doesn't love animals. He's sleeping in the guest room for now."

"Have you talked to him about why he doesn't want a pet?" Sarah sounds thoughtful. "I mean, we all love animals, or we wouldn't be here. But I know people, wonderful people, who really don't get my obsession. Maybe Raymond has a valid reason for not liking them. Like, a guy I know was bitten in the face by a dog when he was a kid. He was afraid of dogs for years, but he would just say he didn't like them."

Patricia tilts her head and thinks. "I guess I should ask him more about why he feels this way. I was so shocked, I didn't know what to say," she snorts, "except the guest room sheets are clean."

"Will you let us know when you do speak to him again?" Bev asks. Patricia agrees, and Bev looks around. "All right, does anyone else have a time they'd like to talk about when they had to overcome negative emotions?"

Oscar raises his hand again. "When *mi madre* passed. That was a very hard time."

"I'm sure it was," Bev says.

"She was sick for a long time with the diabetes and ... what's the word? Kidney sickness. But it wasn't no easier when she died."

"And how did you deal with it?" Bev asks.

Oscar frowns. "I ate." He pauses. "I got bigger, but it got better after a while. I still miss her a lot though."

"Oscar makes a good point." Bev steps to the board again and writes the word *time*. "Time passing can really help when it comes to grief, or any negative emotion."

"And homemade *chilaquiles* and *tacos al pastor* help, too," Oscar adds.

Bev laughs and adds *comfort food* under time. "What else?"

"Good friends help," Sarah says.

Bev writes down *friends*.

"And our Lord," Lydia says. "The only one who can bring true peace and comfort."

Bev writes *faith* on the board. "These are great. What else?"

"I have a very small glass of cordials every evening to help me relax for vespers," Lydia adds. "Father Darnley shares a glass with me when he visits."

Brent nods. "Weed helps."

I practically choke.

Bev hesitates. "I'm aware that we share this space with Alcoholics Anonymous and others working to conquer their addictions. It's possible marijuana and alcohol may not be harmful in small amounts. But I think we have to be very careful about using substances to help cope with negative emotions. Sometimes they mask our feelings rather than helping us to mitigate them."

Brent shrugs. "Helps me."

"Writing things down is helpful," I say. "One day, right after Bailey died, I felt like my head would bust open with all the bad stuff I was feeling. I grabbed a notebook and started writing, and I've kept a journal since then."

Sarah has that thoughtful look on her face again, like she got a peek in my diary. I hope she never does. There's an entry about the fateful poker game in there.

Bev writes *journaling* on the board. "Excellent."

"Reading can help, too," Sarah adds. "I read a few books on grief before signing up for this class. Reading for pleasure distracts me."

Reading goes up on the board.

"And sex," Brent adds. "It's fun and distracting."

I swear if he looks at Sarah, I'm going to punch him, but his eyes stay on the board. Bev hesitates, writes the word *intimacy* on the board, and moves on quickly.

"Grief is a negative emotion, like anger or sadness," she says. "But that doesn't mean it doesn't serve a purpose. The key is to accept it and find ways to cope with it." She points to the list on the board. "These are some ways to do that."

Brent saunters over to Sarah when group ends. She's talking to Lydia, who always takes a while to pack up her Bible, rosary, and ever-present framed picture of Sister Mary Margaret. I keep an eye on Bev, who usually has to rush out to another engagement at the end of our group.

There she and her sandals go.

Brent's standing close to Sarah, his hands in his pockets. I try to evaluate him like a woman might.

He's fit, younger than me by a couple of years, and while I've noticed the front of my hair thinning, he has tons of the stuff. He's a lot more casual than me, too, which doesn't seem to be Sarah's style.

What am I doing? Sarah already told me it wasn't like that with him. And jealousy isn't *my* style. Be cool, Ben.

Once Lydia heads for the elevator, Sarah looks at Brent and me. "You guys ready?"

"Ready for what?" Patricia asks.

Uh-oh. Sarah didn't see Patricia behind her. Will she lie, or will she tell the truth? And if she does tell the truth, will Patricia bust us for breaking the group rules?

Sarah freezes, then finally spits it out. "To Alleycat for coffee. Ben and I went last week on a whim, and Brent joined us. Would you like to go? You're welcome so long as you can keep a secret. Bev's rules and all."

Patricia snorts. "We're adults. We can do whatever we want. Sure, I'll go. I've got no desire to see Raymond right now anyway."

"Let's go already." Brent rubs his stomach. "I'm hungry."

He'd better have money this time. I release an exasperated breath. My intimate coffee date with Sarah last week has somehow become a therapy group after-party.

Great.

Chapter Eleven

Sarah

I'm kind of relieved Brent and Patricia are going for coffee with Ben and me. I could tell I'd put Ben off when I'd told him I was having coffee with Brent again. But having another group date feels safer than going to dinner with Ben.

I can't believe he asked me. And I can't believe my immediate feeling was an enthusiastic yes. Does that make me a glutton for punishment? Or am I just desperate for a wedding date?

Okay, that one is true.

I'm a little worried our extracurricular coffees won't stay secret with four of us going, but too late now. I hoist my giant work tote onto my shoulder. "Let's go."

I feel kind of festive as we walk to Alleycat. I haven't been out with a group of friends in a while. I've been too busy running from appointment to appointment with Ang and Rose, or frankly, sitting at home by myself, missing Sam.

Reclusive. That's what I've been. It's easy to do in the winter in Colorado, especially when you're single. Sam used to get me outside for walks every day at least and a weekly playdate at the dog park. Now, no one needs me to do much of anything except show up for work.

We arrive at Alleycat and snag the table in the corner. It's a little more crowded with four, but we fit. Patricia and I slide onto the bench on one side of the table, leaving Ben and Brent the two chairs on the other side. The cafe is busier than it was last week.

I pull out my wallet. "Can someone grab me a Honey Buzz and one of those brownies I saw in the case on the way in? I can hold the table."

"I got it," Ben and Brent say at the same time.

"I've got it," Ben repeats firmly.

"Sweet," Brent says. "Grab me a coffee and muffin again, then. Thanks, bro." He makes no move to give Ben cash. Ben's eyes narrow.

"Here," I hold out a ten to Ben, "use this."

"No, thanks," he says.

"Would you like anything, Patricia?" Ben asks politely.

She shakes her head, looking confused but also amused. "I don't drink coffee. I'll get myself some tea."

"I'm happy to get it for you. What kind?"

"That's okay. I'll get my own." She follows him to the counter.

Brent grins at me. "That was easy."

"What?"

"Two weeks in a row I scored free coffee and snacks."

My lips thin. "You're buying next week, right?"

He scratches his head. "We'll see. Ben looks like he might be good for one more week."

I roll my eyes. "You're a real gentleman, Brent. Okay, you're going to call Travis this week, right? He has some ideas for you about where you can apply for scholarships and student loans for vet tech school. He said his tech, Amelia, did the same thing before she applied. You can talk to her, too, if you want."

"Yeah, yeah. I'll call them." He's studying the artwork on the ceiling.

I rap the table in front of him, feeling like an old librarian stalking a table of loud teens. "Be sure you do, Brent. This is a good opportunity to talk to someone doing the kind of work you want to do."

He makes a face. "I'm on it. I've got the number. I'll call him."

I do sound like I'm lecturing, or worse, henpecking. But right now, Brent's acting about the same age as those library teens.

"So how was your week?" I ask. "Anything fun happen at the pet store?"

"Yeah, someone accidentally broke one of the fish tanks." He still has his head flopped back over the edge of his chair to better see the ceiling, but he looks up now. "Guppies were everywhere."

I cover my mouth. "Oh no! What did you do?"

"Me? Laughed. It was pretty humorous watching everyone on their hands and knees trying to scoop up the wiggly little guys."

My grouchy librarian voice comes out again. "Brent, you didn't help at all?"

He glances at me. "Sure. But after I had a good laugh first. I was the one who thought to fill a couple of buckets with water so the fish could go in temporarily, until we could get them back in a treated tank."

"That was smart."

Ben and Patricia return with the food and drinks.

"No milk or sugar?" Brent asks when Ben unceremoniously dumps his mug and muffin in front of him, sloshing the coffee.

"You can get your own."

Brent sighs and stands. "Shouldn't a coffee shop have that on the table or something?"

"Could you grab a little extra for me?" I ask.

"I'll get it," Ben says.

Patricia lowers her voice as the two men walk off. "I don't know what all's going on here, but I think we might be seeing why we're not supposed to socialize outside of group."

I try to look innocent. "What do you mean?"

"Sarah, you're younger than me, but you weren't born yesterday. Use your eyes and ears. That Ben likes you."

"No, he doesn't," I answer flatly.

"Mm-hmm. So you say."

She nods meaningfully at me as Ben and Brent both try to be first to put milk and sugar on the table in front of me.

"Thank you," I mumble, avoiding Patricia's eyes. Could Ben like me again . . . still? Or is he trying to prove he's a good guy now?

"So, how's everyone enjoying group?" Patricia asks when no one speaks.

"Better than free YouTube alone at home," Brent says.

When we all nod, it hits me. We're in this grief group because we dearly miss our pets. But . . . I think we're all also there because we're missing something else.

Connection, maybe. People in our lives.

I have Ang and Rose, but they have Julian and Charles more than I have them. If that makes sense.

Patricia has Raymond, but it sounds like they have some communication issues. Oscar has his Edith, but maybe she, I don't know, neglects him because of the *nietos*. And the rest of us? We're alone.

Hmm.

"What will you do about Raymond?" I ask Patricia.

She sits back in her chair. "I don't know. I feel very . . . betrayed . . . maybe? Like he's been hiding this from me."

I nod sympathetically. "I can see that. You thought you understood him, but there's this big thing you don't agree on that you thought you did."

"Yeah, that's about it."

Brent drums his fingers on the table after shoving the last of the muffin in his mouth. He's already drained his coffee.

"What do you think she should do, Brent?" Ben asks.

"About what?"

"Brent!" I say. "About Raymond! Weren't you listening?"

"Nope, not really. What's the problem?"

"Ugh," I say. "Never mind. Ben, what about you? What would you do if you were Patricia?"

He sips his coffee and thinks. "I'd talk to him about it more. See if there's any wiggle room we could agree on. Like maybe he'd be okay with a smaller dog? Or a cat or gerbil or something? I don't know."

Brent turns to Ben, an incredulous look on his face. "Bro, you're gay? You do kind of dress like it, but I thought you were one of those metrosexual types."

Ben smiles. "I'm not gay."

"Oh. I thought since you were saying *him* and all—"

"I was putting myself in Patricia's shoes. You know, taking her perspective? You should try it sometime."

Brent bends down and looks under the table. "Naw, man, her feet are too small. And women's heels look awful, like really uncomfortable. I'm good in my own boots."

The rest of us look at each other but we have no idea what to say to that.

"Those are good ideas, Ben," Patricia says after an awkward pause. "I'll think about it. What about you? Now we know you're not gay," she smirks, "do you have a girlfriend?"

Ben's eyes stay on Patricia and only on Patricia. "No. I haven't for a while."

My heart gives a funny jump.

"Why not?" Patricia asks.

"I dated a few women for a while, but no one was quite right. See, I have this girl in mind that's pretty great. Sweet, spunky, and a good listener."

My mouth goes dry now, too.

"I'm hoping to find one like her." His eyes move to mine, and my face burns hot. I can feel Patricia's eyes on me, too.

"Don't wait too long, bro." Brent points to Ben's head. "You've got some gray hairs up there."

Ben snorts. "Thanks for the advice. Anyway, work and friends have kept me pretty busy the last couple of years."

"And Bailey," I say.

He scratches his head and looks away. "Right, and Bailey took up a lot of time."

Sam's illness and death were all-encompassing last year. I know what that's like. "Has anyone thought about getting another pet?"

Patricia shakes her head. "Uh-uh. Not yet. My Snickers is still too fresh in my head. And now this thing with Raymond? I don't know if I'll ever be able to get another pet. I'll feel like I'm having to choose between my dog and my man. And I don't know if I'll be able to trust that my man likes my dog." Her eyes glitter for a moment, and I touch her arm.

"What about you, Ben?" I ask.

"No, not yet." His faces pinches in an uncomfortable kind of way. Weird.

Brent stares at Ben hard, but only shakes his head. "I would, but I can't afford it yet." He swipes crumbs off the table.

"I thought you had all those frozen rats in your freezer?" Ben says.

"Yeah, but it's not just food. Sev's heat lamp broke, and my ex-girlfriend took his humidifier with her when she took off. There's bedding, too, although I can use a couple of old shirts for a while. The main thing is his terrarium has a crack in it and I need a new one. Twenty-gallon tanks aren't cheap."

"Are you saving up for it?" I ask.

It's Brent's turn to look weird. "Yeah, sure."

After chatting a few more minutes, I yawn and check my watch. "I've got to get home. Early day tomorrow."

I'm trying to get up early and do a YouTube fitness video

every morning this month. I'm doing everything from yoga and Pilates to kickboxing and weightlifting. It's good to switch things up.

"I'll walk you and Patricia to your cars," Ben says.

"Me, too," Brent adds.

We stand and button our coats.

"Don't forget your backpack, Brent," Ben says. He reaches between their chairs to grab it and puts a hand on the bottom as he lifts it. "It's wet."

"Water bottle probably leaked again," Brent says.

We head back to the parking lot behind the church.

"This was nice. Let me know if you go again next week," Patricia says.

"Only if you let us know what happens with Raymond," I say.

"It's a deal." She slides into her Avalon and starts the engine.

"Well, this is me." I gesture to my Honda Civic. "See you guys next week."

"Hey, can I talk to you for a minute?" Ben says to me.

"Sure," I answer. We both glance at Brent.

"Don't let me stop you." He blows on his bare hands. Now that I think about it, he hasn't worn a coat, hat, or gloves to group so far, and while he has a vehicle, it looks like it might seize up, collapse, and go to van heaven any day now.

"Alone," Ben says pointedly at Brent.

"Oh, right. See you two."

Ben waits until Brent fires up his van and sputters out of the lot to speak.

"That guy." He shakes his head.

I laugh. "He's . . . unusual. But I'm used to eccentric people from working at the library. We get all kinds."

"I'll bet." He runs a hand through his hair. "Listen, since the after-party has grown—"

"The what?"

"The after-party. It's what I've started calling it in my head."

"That's a good one. I'm going to borrow it. Anyway, go on."

"Since it's a party of four now, I wanted to see if you'd like to do something with just me this weekend."

My heart rapid fires. Patricia was right, Ben is interested. But how to answer? I can't lie and say that I don't find him attractive anymore. I find him very, very attractive. Like a magnet finds the opposite pole of another magnet attractive. But . . . I don't trust him. I firmly believe that someone who lies once can and probably will lie again.

"I don't know," I say.

"Listen, Sarah, I know things didn't end all that well for us in college."

I adjust the straps on my tote bag and give him a look. "You think?"

"But I'd really appreciate it if you gave me another chance." He shifts his feet. "That girl I described back at the cafe? It was you."

I bite my lip. "It was?"

"Yeah. I'd love to get to know you better—again."

I still hesitate. What's different now? Ben's older and presumably more mature, but he didn't seem all that immature back in college until I caught him still dating his ex when he said he wasn't. So how can I trust him now?

Ben touches my hand. "C'mon, it'll be fun. We can reminisce about the good old days."

"College?" I say skeptically.

"If you want. Or, scratch that, we won't mention CSU. It's off the table. Dogs, too, if you want."

"Dogs are *never* off the table," I joke. "Sam was on mine all the time, whenever I left a chair pulled out a little too far."

He laughs, but he looks kind of weird again. "So? What do you think?"

I imagine how I'd feel saying yes, then saying no. But before I can feel the feelings all the way, the word yes comes out of my mouth. Traitorous tongue.

He grins. "Great. How about Saturday?"

"Oh, sorry, I'm working."

"Then Sunday?" he asks. I nod. "Can I get your number? I'll text you."

I tell him my number. But I squirm a little as I do. Is this a good idea? I'm not sure this is a good idea. Mainly because of Ben, but also, "What happens if Bev finds out?"

"She won't. It's a lot riskier to go out for coffee right after group than to do something over the weekend."

"That's true. But somehow that feels less like we're breaking the rules. Two-thirds of the group is there anyway."

Ben scratches his head. "Are we really that worried about breaking our support group rules?"

I think of what Rose said. "I guess not."

"So, I'll see you this weekend."

"Okay." I muster a smile and open my car door. His eyes stay on me another few seconds, and then he heads for his car.

I have another date with Ben Becker.

I have another date with Ben Becker!

My whole body buzzes, but my heart might as well be shaking its head with disgust. It gives me pause.

Can I really trust him this time? Or will he give me a second Black Lie?

Chapter Twelve

Ben

Sarah isn't sure she can trust me—that's clear. But I'm still pumped she agreed to go out with me.

I can't go home yet. My blood's charging around my body, and I'm grinning like a fool. I turn the music down and call my brother, Adam, as I drive aimlessly through town. He's in graduate school at University of Colorado Denver, and he works at a restaurant in his spare time. I'm pretty sure he's off tonight, though.

We catch up for a few minutes, then I say, "Hey, I have a date."

Normally, that wouldn't be something I'd call home about, but when I tell him who it's with, Adam gets it. He remembers how bad I felt about how that all went down.

"Where did you meet her this time?" he asks.

I tell him. "And she still works at a library. Old Town."

"Does she wear glasses like Tina Fey? Sexy librarian vibe and all?"

I laugh. "No, not really. I mean, I think she's great looking but different than Tina Fey."

To tell the truth, Sarah doesn't look like a lot of other women I've dated. Back in college, I used to go for leggy blondes. Sort of the typical hot girl. But I dated one too many that were full of themselves, had some kind of agenda, or weren't honest with me about how they felt.

"And she was okay with why you went to the group to begin with?" Adam says. I don't answer. "Wait—you haven't told her? Dude, are you serious?"

"I know, I know. But I just got her to go out with me. How do I even bring it up?"

"There's not going to be a convenient segue into this, Ben. You'll have to blurt it out. 'Sarah, I joined the group to cover a poker debt. I don't have a dog. I can't be around dogs. When I'm around dogs, my face swells up like a tick, and I choke on my own tongue.'"

"It's not that bad. And I can't say all that."

"Of course not. You say it your way."

What is my way? "I'll figure it out."

"Make sure you do. And soon. If you don't, and she finds out, this is going to go very badly."

"I know. Thanks, brother."

"No problem. Call me later."

When I hang up, I realize I'm close to the foothills. They're as black as the night sky, but I can sort of feel them out there lurking in front of me. I pull into the parking lot of some commercial building, turn the engine off, and stare up at the stars.

This date with Sarah feels more important than just any date. I know I need to be honest with her, but I also think she might forgive me more easily once she knows me better. Again.

I'll tell her. I will. But . . . maybe not quite yet.

Chapter Thirteen

Sarah

The dining room of the Pine Mountain Inn, wedding venue extraordinaire north of Fort Collins, is almost as exquisite on a regular old Thursday evening as it is fully decked out in twinkle lights for a July wedding. I would know, I've been here twice, once as the MOH.

The inn is an old Victorian house that's been converted to an event space. A building was built in the back for outside weddings and parties, and the house holds the kitchen and several rooms for smaller events. The style is modern farmhouse, I'd say.

"Are you ready for this?" Ang asks me.

"Can't wait," I say. "What about you, Julian?"

"I'm starving."

I actually hear his stomach growl.

"Baby, I told you to eat something before you came. This is a tasting, not a full meal. Remember?" Ang looks part exasperated, part amused. She sometimes treats Julian like a naughty child. He doesn't object.

"I skipped lunch so I could work out. You don't want a flabby fiancé up there next to you, do you?"

"Thank you for thinking of me. You're so sweet. But I don't care about that; I only want you." Ang kisses Julian, and they whisper something to each other and laugh.

And . . . there's the longing again. I wish I had someone to nuzzle and whisper with, too. I don't let myself consider Ben.

A memory hits me broadside. Sam and me on the couch, watching a romantic movie that inevitably brings tears. Although I'd made little sound, and he'd been dead asleep, he woke with a start and zeroed in on me. Somehow, without getting to his feet, he wiggled over to me and put his heavy head on my leg for a minute before slipping all the way into my lap. He then licked my damp cheek once or twice, whined, and watched me anxiously.

I mean, what human can compete with that?

But Sam's gone. And while I don't think anyone, human or canine, can take his place, I can't give up on living.

"Sarah, hon, what's wrong? You're crying." Ang has her hand on the back of my chair, and Julian's expression is concerned.

I dive into my bag for Kleenex; I keep a pack close by at all times for such an occasion. "Ugh, memories."

"Sam again?" she asks. Sam still? I can tell she wants to say.

"I know, I should be over him." She doesn't get it, like Bev was talking about in group. But Ben does, a voice in my head whispers. My pulse picks up.

"Maybe your date this weekend will help," Ang says slyly.

"Hold up, no one told me anything about a date. Who is it? Do I need to do a background check?" Julian works for the city as a planner, but he claims to have access to the state bureau of investigation database.

"Julian, you know that's illegal," Ang turns her stink eye on him.

"And worth it in this case. We need to know who Sarah's getting involved with."

I hold up my hands, laughing. "It's okay, Julian, I knew him in college."

"He could have killed someone in the last five years. Or worse."

I make a face. "What's worse than killing someone?"

"I don't know, but we're damn sure gonna find out."

Ang and I laugh. I'm grateful to my friends for hauling me back up out of the dark pit I sometimes fall into.

Maggie, the catering manager, staggers in with an oval silver tray covered by a lid. Getting to help choose the tasting menu is yet another perk of the MOH position. In fact, seriously, why do I complain about it? This gig is phenomenal.

"Now. Before we get started, has everyone washed their hands?" Maggie pulls a small bottle of hand sanitizer out and offers it to us with a wide smile.

She's maybe mid-thirties, skinny-limbed, and diminutive, like a bird. A bird with a tuft of golden-red hair on top. Her blue eyes shift nervously behind absolutely enormous glasses that only contribute to the avian impression.

I hadn't met her until today, but Ang told me all about her. My friend throws me a hint of a grin now.

"We washed before we came in," Julian says with a sigh.

"Um, I didn't." Ang elbows me. I did wash. I want to see what Maggie will do.

"Oh! Hands, please." She squirts the clear liquid in my palm, and I rub my hands together. "I have to be mindful of food safety in my job. Can't be too careful."

I have a hard time not snorting. How disgusting does she think we are?

Maggie speaks to Ang and Julian. "I know you aren't interested in a sit-down meal at the reception and instead would like to do food stations and passed hors d'oeuvres."

Ang nods and squeezes Julian's hand. "We want to be able to

drink and dance and visit with all our family and friends instead of being up at the main table like wedding peacocks, while people like my favorite aunt Michelle and cousin Marcus are stuck in the back."

Julian raises an eyebrow. "I don't know, we might want Marcus to stay in the back."

Ang swats him. "He's only seven. But we won't have to worry about him anyway with a stand-up style reception. He can dance and run around, and he won't interrupt anyone. Much."

"Are you sure?" Maggie says.

Ang's forehead wrinkles. "About which part?"

"The food stations. You do know that increases the risk of spreading disease as they're open to sneezing, coughing, touching the food . . ." Maggie shudders.

"But—you offer that option in your catering services," Julian says.

"I wish we wouldn't. I've debated with the owner about it on many occasions. I even showed her educational videos about the spread of germs at large public events like weddings, but she doesn't listen."

"I'm sure those videos must be riveting," Julian says.

"They are! You have no idea how fascinating, and disgusting, those things can be . . ." Maggie trails off. She's eyeing Ang and Julian's still-clasped hands. She holds out the bottle of sanitizer, and without a word, they hold out their palms for a squirt. Maggie nods and flips the top shut with a sharp snap.

"I think we'll take our chances with the stations," Ang says.

"Well, if you're sure, then you're in luck. We have a very special hors d'oeuvres menu. It's delicious and absolutely gorgeous." Maggie removes the lid on the tray with a flourish. "This is our signature oysters Rockefeller appetizer."

The oysters—sitting in rock salt, covered in a sprinkling of cheese, breadcrumbs, and some other delicious looking bits, and garnished with parsley and lemon—look divine. We all reach for a plate, but Maggie squeaks before we actually touch them. "Be careful!"

Julian rolls his eyes. "With what?"

"The sharp edges on the shells! I had a client cut themselves once."

I peer at the oyster shell after gingerly selecting one from the platter. "Really? That seems hard to do."

"Trust me, it happened. And please be careful swallowing, don't choke now."

Her hands twist together in front of her. I practically choke thanks to trying to suck down an oyster while not laughing. Once my friends and I successfully swallow our food, something we've done perfectly safely for at least thirty years, Maggie clears the small plates and puts three clean ones in front of us.

"We can reuse those first plates," I point out.

Maggie's lips thin into white lines. She looks horrified by the suggestion. "Fresh plates for every course are a food safety standard."

Ang throws me a look—don't get her started. "Okay, you were right. The oysters were delicious. What's up next?"

"Next is our vegetable and couscous salad. It's a lovely option for your vegetarian guests." She places a second platter, handed to her by an assistant who scurries back to the kitchen, down in front of us and scoops out a portion for each of us. "This is a medley of roasted vegetables—eggplant, beets, zucchini, and peppers on a bed of mixed greens and couscous. It's divine."

We each separate out a bite with our forks and knives, and I'm about to pop the salad in my mouth when Maggie squeaks and throws her hand at me.

"Wait! I forgot to ask if you have any nut allergies! This dish has a sprinkle of pine nuts."

"No nut allergy," I say before closing my mouth over the fork.

Maggie puts the hand on her chest and closes her eyes. "Thank goodness. I'd asked Angela and Julian in our first appointment, but I never asked you."

It's difficult to see how this woman gets any second appointments at all.

I take the opportunity of her talking to taste the couscous. It's also scrumptious. I guess this is why she gets return customers. The reputation of the food and service at the Pine Mountain Inn is top-notch.

I nod at my friends. "That one was wonderful, too."

Maggie looks delighted. "Wait until you try our lobster and mashed potatoes and the filet mignon with roasted green beans." She gestures at the next tray coming in.

What safety concerns will she warn us about next? Obviously, the lobster could somehow still be alive after being boiled and claw our eyes out. The filet is a little more difficult to imagine. I've got it: the green beans are clearly choking hazards.

My nerves are shot by the time we get to the figs with bacon and *chile* and the caviar and *crème fraîche* tartlets, but my stomach is in the promised land.

Maggie provides Ang and Julian a list of the different dishes we'd tried, and we stand to leave. Honestly, I'm shocked the woman didn't make us wipe down our chairs. She probably does that herself.

"Please be careful walking down the stairs," she says as we say goodbye.

"We'll do our best," Julian mutters.

After the front door of the inn closes behind us, Ang and I burst out laughing.

"She's a trip, isn't she?" she asks.

"I can definitely see why her food gets such amazing reviews," I say. "And why no one ever gets sick from it."

"She insists on having hand sanitizer pumps on every food station and table at weddings, but at least she wraps them in ribbon or something. She showed me, they're kind of pretty." She shakes her head.

"Well, ladies, I need to get back to town," Julian says. "I'm meeting Don for a drink."

Ang grabs his arm. "Be careful. Don't, I don't know, drop a cocktail glass. It might shatter, and you could cut your foot."

He kisses her. "Not a chance."

I tilt my head and try to look nervous, like Maggie. "I mean, there is a chance. There's also a chance you could fall off your barstool and break your neck."

He shakes his head. "There was a chance that lobster would hop off the plate and sing 'Under the Sea' with the filet, but it didn't happen."

As he takes off in his car, I turn to Ang. I drove us up from the library.

"Where to?" I ask.

"Do you have a few minutes? I have something to show you."

"Absolutely."

"Back to the library then. It's in my car."

Over the twenty-minute ride, I tell her the latest with my group, the coffee after-party, and more about my upcoming date with Ben. I'd only had a minute at work earlier to fill her in about it.

"I'm so happy for you, Sarah! Now you won't have to go solo to my wedding." She nudges me, and I roll my eyes.

"Let's not get too far ahead of ourselves. Ben and I haven't even had a real date yet. At least not one that wasn't crashed by several members of our grief group."

"Where are you two going?" she asks.

"He hasn't told me. But he texted to ask if eight o'clock Sunday morning works."

"That early? Seriously? And you didn't ask what you were doing?"

"Of course, I did. He said it's a surprise."

"Do you have an exit plan?"

I glance at her. "Do I need an exit plan?"

"What if it goes terribly wrong and you need an excuse of somewhere to be?"

"What could go terribly wrong at eight in the morning?"

"Sarah, I mean it."

I put on my left turn signal. "I'll text you a secret code."

"What code?" she asks. "So I can be on the lookout."

I think about it. "'Under the Sea.' And when you get that, you'll call me to let me know that you've had a terrible gardening accident, or a mad cow rampaged through your house, or you were attacked by your oatmeal."

Ang hoots. "I'll have my phone ready. And you have to let me know where you go. This is so mysterious."

My skin tingles with nervous anticipation as I drive the last few minutes to the library. I've dated guys the last few years, but the dates felt increasingly . . . casual. Like we were only killing time together until something—or more specifically someone—better came along.

This date with Ben feels like it could be more than that.

I pull beside Ang's car in the library parking lot and turn off the engine. She gets out, digs in her glove box, then gets back in with—

"A box of tampons? That's what you wanted to show me?" I ask.

"That's right. I wanted to make sure you knew what to do with these." She rolls her eyes. "No, it's this."

She opens the box top and slides out a slim hardcover book. It's *The Dream Keeper* by Langston Hughes. I take it carefully. It's clearly old, with a worn but still beautiful navy cloth cover and gold print for the title. Two large stars poise on either side of the word "the."

"It's a first edition from 1932." Her voice is a whisper.

"Ang, it's stunning. Wow."

"It's my wedding gift for Julian. I searched all over the internet and finally found this last week."

I swallow hard thinking about the significance of the gift. Ang and Julian met at a poetry reading at a mutual friend's house in Boulder. They're both amateur poets, and they fell for each other over their shared love of Langston Hughes, Maya Angelou, and other brilliant African American poets.

"He's going to love it. What an amazing, thoughtful gift." I hand it back to her and hug her. "He's so lucky to be getting you for a wife."

"Not as lucky as I am to be getting him for a husband." She slides the book back into the tampon box.

"Um, Ang? Why the box?"

"I'm hiding it from him of course." She points at me. "Do you know the one thing a man won't touch? Your tampon box. Trust me."

I burst out laughing. Maybe I can smuggle my Prozac bottle, a recent addition to my life since Sam died, into my own herd of tampons, in case Ben uses my bathroom when he comes to pick me up.

Hey, it could totally work. Unless, along with being mendacious, Ben Becker is a snoop.

Lying is one thing. Snooping is another. If he paws through my tampon box, it's clearly over.

Chapter Fourteen

Sarah

Ben arrives promptly at eight in the morning on Sunday. I smooth my perfectly hemmed, straight leg jeans, zip up my fitted teal hoodie, and check my lipstick before answering the door.

He'd texted yesterday to wear clothes and shoes comfortable for walking outdoors, which presented a serious wardrobe problem. I usually prefer skirts or dresses with tights and boots in winter, especially for a date. How do you dress for a first date—that is, looking as cute as possible—while also dressing for exercise?

After a consultation with Ang, I decided on my jeans, cutest sneakers, and the hoodie. It's a high-low style, so it drapes over my butt, and Rose tells me the color of the sweatshirt transforms my blue eyes to virtually emerald green. Dressing casually also means I had to keep the styling of my hair and makeup light, but I did my best to make everything pop.

I open the door to find Ben in well-fitting joggers and a puffer coat. He's wearing winter gloves and a hat, too.

I refuse to cover this recently styled head with a hat. My curls are hard to tame on the best of days, but they're nearly perfect today, not frizzy and not droopy either. I don't mind covering my hands, I guess, even though I did give myself a manicure last night for the occasion.

"Hey! Come on in while I grab my mittens," I say.

He steps inside and pulls his hat off, which gives him a sexy bedhead look that I can't quite tear my eyes away from at first. But I finally fish in the basket in my coat closet where I keep gloves, hats, and scarves, while Ben looks around.

"Wow." I hear him mutter.

I pull my head out of the closet. "What?"

He's looking at the pictures of Sam lining the entryway. There's Sam enjoying a swim in a mountain lake. He loved the water. Next to that is a pic of Sam knocked out on his dog bed in a patch of sun. And another of Sam running full tilt across a snow-covered meadow.

I cringe. At least Ben can't see my bedroom. He might really worry about me then.

"He was so darn photogenic. I couldn't help myself," I say.

"That wasn't why I said wow," Ben says. "I expected photos of Sam."

"Oh. Why did you then?"

"Your place is as clean as my grandmother's mouth. And she brushes and flosses twice a day and goes to church twice a week."

I smile, still a little embarrassed, and pull my coat off a hanger. "I have a lot of time on my hands these days."

"I get it." He nods at my cold weather gear. "Are you ready?"

"All set."

He leans in and kisses my cheek. "You look beautiful, by the way."

He turns to get the door before I can respond, which is probably for the best since my face flames like a sudden wildfire.

I touch the spot on my cheek. That was the nicest, most

casually sincere compliment a first date has ever given me. Not that I've had all that many. I decide to be bold.

I lock my front door and reach Ben as he opens the passenger door for me. I catch his hand and hold it in mine.

"Thank you. That was really sweet."

He rubs the back of my hand with his thumb for a moment and then helps me into the car.

I sneak a peek of myself in the side-view mirror. So much for trying to achieve the perfect touch with my makeup. My face is so pink from embarrassment, I look like a geranium.

Speaking of flowers, Rose and Miss P peep out from behind her floral curtains as I buckle my seatbelt. I wave at them, and Rose waves with Petunia's paw before disappearing.

"Now can I ask where we're going so early on a Sunday?" I say as Ben starts the car.

"It's not far." He smiles at me.

"That did not answer my question."

"And yet, it's the only one you're going to get for the moment," he says playfully.

We drive south on Highway 287 toward Loveland. The foothills, lit by the morning sun, are to our right. They look particularly spectacular today with the blue sky outlining them and snow frosting the higher peaks.

My plan was to be cool, maybe even a little aloof, and make Mr. Hang Me Out to Lie prove himself. But after he complimented me, I'm suddenly feeling shy. Ben seems content to drive with only the radio playing softly in the background.

"Where does your brother live now?" I finally ask. "His name is Adam, right?"

"He's getting his MBA down at CU Denver."

"Do you see him much?"

"Yeah, we get together at least once a month to play poker with some friends." His hands tighten on the wheel, and his knuckles briefly go white. Huh, I wonder why?

"What about your family?" he asks. "How are they?"

I tell him about my sister, Liz, and my parents and grandparents back in Omaha.

"Do you ever think about going back to Nebraska?" he asks.

I gesture at the mountains. "I miss my people, but I don't think I could do it. I love my job, my friends, and Colorado too much."

"Yeah, me, too. My company has better paying positions in other places, but I can't see leaving here."

It's good to know we agree on that. When, if, I meet someone I want to marry, I really want to raise my family here. It's a great quality of life.

After about fifteen minutes, when we get to Loveland and he shows no sign of stopping, I ask again where we're going.

He smiles and looks sidelong at me. "Longmont."

Longmont is a town between Fort Collins and Boulder. There are lots of great restaurants and breweries there, but surely, we aren't going to one of them at the crack of dawn on a Sunday? Breakfast maybe? But then, why the walking clothes? I give up trying to guess his plan.

Twenty minutes later or so, we make our way into what looks like a quiet, suburban neighborhood of Longmont. Except . . . there seems to be a lot of activity for a Sunday morning. Cars line the residential streets, and people with lots and lots of dogs walk up and down the sidewalks.

Ben pulls into a nearly full middle school parking lot and turns to me. "Okay, I know this isn't a traditional first date kind of thing. But this also isn't actually our first date."

He points at the people climbing out of cars and trying to corral excited dogs of all sizes. I catch sight of a yellow Lab lumbering along beside its owner, and my chest tightens.

"Today's the annual Longmont Critter Crawl. I thought, since I know you're missing Sam, that we could get some quality time with other people's dogs for a few hours. And it goes to a good cause, the Longmont Animal Shelter."

Suddenly, the early time frame makes all kinds of sense. And the idea . . . "I think it's a perfect not-first date, Ben."

He grins. "Come on. I already registered us, so we're good to go."

We join the throng and head for the banner that shows the starting area. It looks like we'll walk along a greenway with great views of the mountains. It's definitely cool; I'm glad I grabbed my mittens and a coat after all.

A man talks excitedly over a loudspeaker, giving an update of when the walk will start, but it's hard to hear much over the excited barks, whines, and squeals of the canine crowd.

Dogs of all shapes and sizes, and their owners, mill around the school. My biggest challenge is deciding which dog to greet first. There's a German shepherd, pointy ears perked at all the noise, a boxer that seems to have springs in its feet, and three Chihuahuas barking nonstop in their owner's arms. I pet each in turn. The boxer tries to lick my face off, and I can't stop smiling. Ben sneezes several times.

"Are you okay?" I ask.

He nods. "I have some allergies. I'm fine."

As we mill around, greeting tons of other dogs, an aquamarine RV catches my eye. I grab Ben's arm. "Oh! Doctor Travis and Amelia are here!"

His brow quirks. "The vet?"

"Let's go say hi!"

We wind through the crowd to the vehicle with the Love & Pets Mobile Animal Clinic logo on the side. Travis and Amelia stand outside, holding pugs on leashes. His dark hair is loose today, falling to his shoulders, while Amelia's bright blonde mane is braided. He has on black scrubs with a puffer coat, while Amelia wears aqua to match the RV. She sees me coming first.

"Sarah! I didn't know you'd be here!"

"Neither did I." I hug her, and Travis, too. After a year of fighting Sam's cancer with these two, they feel more like family.

I introduce them to Ben, and then I greet Doug and Daisy,

their precious pugs. The dogs' tails wag furiously, and they make soft snorting noises followed by a quick bark each.

"Are you in Fort Collins, too?" Travis asks Ben.

Ben nods. "Sarah and I met in college, and we recently reconnected."

"That's great!" Amelia says with a quick glance at me that tells me she guesses we're on a date. I blush; the cat's out of the bag now. So to speak. Her face lights up. "Would you want to take Doug and Daisy with you on the walk? They could use the exercise, and we can really use the time to get ready for our appointments after everyone gets back."

"We'd love to!" I look at Ben. "I mean, I'd love to. Is that okay with you, Ben?"

When he agrees without hesitating, Travis and Amelia hand us the leashes. "Don't let them get away from you. They're runners. Especially Doug."

Doug nudges Daisy with his blunt nose as if to say, Yeah, we are.

"They are so sweet," I say. Right then, Daisy growls and snaps at Doug. Not a real bite, a warning, but still.

I laugh. "I spoke too soon."

Travis shakes his head. "She gets annoyed with him sometimes, especially when there's a lot going on."

"We'll take good care of them," I say. "Thanks for letting us borrow them."

"Thank *you*," Travis says. "Hang on to them for as long as you want, then bring them back here when you get sick of them."

We say goodbye and wander toward the start banner again.

"One minute until the kickoff of the 2020 Critter Crawl. Ladies and gentlemen, two legged and four legged and everything between, start your engines!" The announcer sounds like he can't imagine anything more thrilling.

A horn blasts, the throng of people and dogs surge, and Doug and Daisy pull us forward.

I catch Ben's eye. "Thank you so much for planning this. I needed it."

He rubs my back with his free hand. "I was hoping you'd feel that way."

I'm starting to feel other ways, too, even if I shouldn't. About Ben. He's been nothing but sweet, considerate, and thoughtful this morning. The choice of what to do on our date alone shows me he really tried to think about what I might enjoy doing.

If things continue like this, I can imagine being head over tail about Ben Becker in short order.

Again.

Chapter Fifteen

Ben

As Sarah, Doug, Daisy, and I amble along the two-mile course, I'm feeling pretty good about things. This is going better than expected.

It was a gamble, taking a woman to a charity dog walking event on our not-first date, but it was one I thought I could pull off. I mean, we met in a pet grief support group.

Still, I wasn't sure if she might be offended or think it was a dumb idea. From the happy smile on her face as we walk, I shouldn't have worried. And her happiness makes me happy. I'm glad I got those allergy shots this week, though. I'm only holding off the scratching, sneezing, and swelling by letting Sarah do all the petting and being really careful not to touch my face.

Doug and Daisy keep us busy by sniffing every canine butt they pass, and Sarah takes the opportunity to say hello to the dogs and their owners, too. She spends extra-long with the Labs we see. And there are a lot if you include mixes. Chocolate, yellow, black, and even one silver Lab that the owner says is a variation of a chocolate.

Even though it's clear she's having fun, the sadness in Sarah's eyes when she pets the Labs is hard to miss. I try hard to remember I'm supposed to be equally sad about Bailey.

I can normally walk two miles in a little over twenty minutes. These two miles take an hour, but it's worth it. We get back to the starting area where music plays and tents are set up with all kinds of animal-related products. The Love & Pets RV seems to have a steady stream of traffic.

I spot an empty bench. "Want to sit for a few minutes?"

Sarah agrees, and we grab it. Doug and Daisy don't hesitate, they jump right into our laps and settle down for the first time since I've met them. I stiffen and keep my head as far away from Doug as possible. I don't want my nose to start running.

"So, Travis and Amelia used to drive up to Fort Collins to see Sam?" I ask.

"About once a month. They have other patients there, too. I'd meet them for appointments in Denver or other places if I had time. Who was Bailey's vet?"

I panic for a second. I haven't been to a vet in Fort Collins. A recent casual conversation with a coworker saves me. She said she'd taken her sick, older dog to— "The CSU vet school. They have great specialists." That's what my colleague said anyway. I hope it's true.

"They do. I took Sam there for an oncology consult."

I nod, relieved. Dodged a bullet there.

"But who was your regular vet?" Sarah asks after a second.

I busy myself with rearranging my beanie. "Um, that one on College? I'm blanking on the name." But I'm pretty sure I've seen a couple of vet clinics on College.

"Aspen Grove?" Sarah says.

"That's it."

"I've heard good things about it."

I nod again. I don't want to embellish any more than I have to.

Sarah scratches Daisy, who responds by licking her hand. "What did you feed Bailey?"

I groan inside at piling lie on lie, but at least this question is easier to field. "He ate anything. So, whatever was on sale at the grocery store." That was all technically true. Except my parents bought the food. Guilt throbs in my temples.

Sarah tucks a lock of hair behind her ear. I watch her, wanting to do it myself. Her hair is a beautiful shade of brown, like a chocolate Lab's, now that I think about it, and curly. I've never dated a woman with curls like hers. Well, except for Sarah herself.

"How did Bailey die?" she asks. "You never said."

At least I don't have to lie about this one. "His back went out. I think they technically called it a ruptured disc. He was too old to operate on it, so they had to put him to sleep."

Even years later, I can feel the sorrow of that day. I did love that dog. Even though my allergies kept my parents from getting any more pets, Adam and I had great childhoods in part because of Bailey.

"I miss him." And I really feel it.

Sarah listens quietly, only her mittened hand moving as she pets a snoozing Daisy. Doug snores in my lap. I guess two miles, plus the thrill of all the dog butts, people, and food smells were too much for these little guys.

"Did you have any dogs growing up?" I ask.

"Yes. All Labs. My parents loved them, too."

"How many have you had?"

"Well, there was George first, a chocolate, but I barely remember him. He died when I was five. He was supposedly very loyal and very protective. My parents said when they would put me in my crib, he wouldn't leave my room until they came to get me out the next morning. They said it drove my older sister, Liz, crazy. She wanted to play with him."

I scratch my nose without thinking, and sneeze. Both dogs jump. We laugh and get them settled again.

"Then we got Stella," Sarah says. "She was the dog I really grew up with. Liz, Stella, and I did everything together. We made forts in the woods behind our house. We swam in the backyard pool when Dad wasn't around to yell at us about cleaning it out if we were going to take Stella swimming in it. And we told Stella all our secrets. I cried more than once into her fur over a boy." She sighs. "I loved that dog. I cried so much when she died, my parents thought they were going to have to take me to see a therapist. I guess I shouldn't have been surprised about being so distraught over Sam." She smooths Daisy's folded ears between her fingers and thumb. The pug sighs in her sleep.

"My parents got Linus after that. He's a sweet black Lab, but I only lived with him for two years before I left for college, and I was so busy." She looks out at the tumble of dogs and people. "Sam was my college graduation present from my parents. I really missed having a dog those four years."

She smiles at me, but tears sparkle in her eyes. One escapes, and I watch as she wipes it away. My eyes fall to her lips.

I've thought about kissing Sarah pretty much every day since I re-met her. We shared a few over the short time we dated, and I remember them being amazing. Is it too soon to kiss her now?

I lean over and touch my lips to hers. I mean to stop there, to give her a little room to think about if she wants me to kiss her again, but right away Sarah pulls my mouth to hers, kissing me this time.

Surprised, I tense for a split second, but then settle into it. She tastes sweet, like cherry cola. Does she use that flavor of ChapStick or something? I wish I weren't wearing gloves so I could finally run my hands through her hair. I think about tearing them off, but it doesn't seem like the thing to do at nine in the morning in a public park. Until Sarah pulls her mittens off and buries her hands in *my* hair.

I do the same, taking my time exploring her soft curls with my hand, her mouth with my lips. She feels so good. Drawn to her warmth, I move closer.

Too close. The dogs get squashed.

Daisy startles awake and growls at Doug. Doug barks.

Daisy spills off Sarah's lap, Doug follows, and leashes trailing, the pugs rocket across the sidewalk and into the crowd.

Chapter Sixteen

Sarah

My eyes go from fifty percent closed and one hundred percent swoony to wide open and panicked in a nanosecond.

"Let's go!" I yell.

Ben and I tear after the pugs . . . who are causing quite a stir. They charge through groups of people and dogs, barking and howling like a surreal sequel to *Braveheart* with pugs.

Terriers are terrified, a Husky hustles out of their way, and a bulldog bravely bulldozes his owner to the side to avoid them. The startled man yells at the pugs after he spills his drink all over his shirt.

Ben pulls ahead of me. I try to keep up, but he's very fast. Unfortunately, Doug and Daisy are faster. I try to stay focused on the pugs, but I can't breathe, and I'm getting a cramp. I don't do a lot of running.

Amelia told me the story of how she finally got together with Travis. Doug, who was her dog initially, ran away during the first annual Love & Pets Party, a pet-centric community event that

Travis and Amelia organize every year in August. Travis got Doug back by playing a song Doug loves. Which gives me an idea . . .

"I'll go get Travis and Amelia," I yell to Ben. "You keep after them!"

Ben waves as acknowledgement. I'm tempted to stop and watch him for a moment. He's very fit, isn't he . . .?

Stay focused, Sarah. First, *breathe*. Then, Travis and Amelia.

I beeline for the RV. The door's closed. I hear voices inside, so I knock, and then say, "Travis? Amelia? I'm sorry to interrupt, but Doug and Daisy ran off!"

The door opens, and Amelia pokes her head out, her eyebrows knitted together. "Sarah? What happened?"

Travis appears behind her holding the oddest-looking Persian cat. It has beautiful silver fur but huge, droopy green eyes and a severe underbite. Yet, somehow, it still has a regal air about it. I stare for a second before remembering the pugs. How to explain the problem? So, Ben and I were kind of making out on a bench, and—

"Daisy and Doug, they . . . chased a squirrel. They have their leashes on and Ben's following them, but I wondered if you could have the DJ play the song? The one Doug loves?"

Amelia and Travis share a smile.

"I'm on it," he says.

He passes the Persian to Amelia and hurries past me toward the DJ's tent where the speakers pump out music. Amelia gives the cat to a tall, slim woman who steps into view from the back of the RV. She has waist length, sunset red-gold hair, pale skin, and her sweat suit is pure princess pink. The owner is as remarkable as her cat.

"I'm so sorry, Kathleen," Amelia says. "We'll be right back to see Klara." She steps out of the RV, and we follow Travis to the DJ.

"What song is it that Doug loves?" I ask her.

Amelia scans the crowd for the dogs, and then glances at me.

"Do you remember that one, 'Girl, I Love You So Bad' by Lil' Dougie? It was really popular a few years ago."

"I do." It was the hot summer hip-hop song. "Why does he love it?"

She laughs. "Now, that's a long story. I'll tell you sometime."

Ahead of us, Travis talks to the DJ, who stops the music. "Folks, we've got some renegade pugs. They're wearing leashes and tags, and their names are Doug and Daisy. If you see them, grab their leashes. Meanwhile, here's a recent favorite from Lil' Dougie."

The song starts playing. Amelia and I reach the tent and join Travis.

"I'm so sorry," I tell them. "Doug and Daisy had a great time on the walk. We were taking a break after it when they, er, ran."

Amelia pats my back. "It's okay. We'll find them. If this doesn't work, nothing will." But she bites her lip and leans into Travis, who puts an arm around her.

"At least they're together," he says. "If one was gone, the other would freak out."

I fidget and bite a nail as the song plays and we wait. People go back to milling around and talking, their dogs sniffing butts and playing together. Right when I think the idea isn't going to work, I see Ben coming our way, a pug under each arm.

My hero.

Doug and Daisy pant, their eyes as scrunched as their sweet faces, but otherwise they look no worse for the wear. Ben puts them down, holding their leashes firmly.

"They're slippery little suckers," he says. "I caught Daisy first, but she snaked out of my grasp. Then, Doug stopped short, tilted his head like he heard something, turned straight around, and tore back this way. I grabbed Daisy's leash again on the way by, and Doug came back to her."

Travis laughs and takes the leash ends. "Sounds about right."

"Thank you for chasing them down," Amelia says.

"I'm really very sorry, again, that we let them get away," I say.

"No harm done," Travis says, "but we should get back to our patient. I'll call you soon about your friend, Brent."

Travis and Amelia head back to the RV, a pug leash in each hand, and I put my face in my hands, laughing. After a second, Ben laughs, too.

"Dating rule number one," I say as we wander away from the DJ booth. "Don't kiss with pugs in your laps."

Ben takes my hand and steps closer, still grinning. "What about without pugs? Any rules there?"

My breath catches as he draws me to a stop. "No, none I can think of."

"Good." His eyes grow serious.

When his mouth finds mine again, and my insides turn to molten lava, I wonder how I've lived the last six years without kissing Ben Becker. Everyone should try it at least once.

But as he pulls me close to deepen our kiss, he suddenly spins away and lets loose a tremendous sneeze, followed by three more. When he finally stands upright and turns back to me, his eyes are red and watery, and his nose is running. His face even looks a little puffy.

I try to find some tissue in my pocket. "Are you okay?"

Muttering something about his allergies and blowing his nose, he rushes off toward the restrooms. Puzzled, I watch him go.

How in the world did Ben live with Bailey when he has such terrible reactions to dogs?

Chapter Seventeen

Ben
Lost Paws, Session Four

And finally, it's Tuesday. When I'll see Sarah, and we'll probably hang out at the after-party. The group time couldn't come soon enough. All I've wanted for the last two days was to be with her again.

I'm in my seat early. Brent comes in first and collapses in his chair. "Hey, bro. How was your weekend?"

I imagine nonchalantly saying, I had a date with Sarah. How do you like them apples?

But I'm not an immature jerk. So, instead I say, "Good. How was yours?"

"Amazing. I had a hot date with that chick, Sarah." He jerks a thumb at her empty seat across the circle.

I sit up so quick I shoot my chair backwards a few inches. "What? When?" Was it Saturday, when she'd *said* she had to work?

He stares at me for a second and then smirks. "You've got it bad for that girl, huh?"

I don't answer. I'm pretty sure I've gone stop-sign-red in the face. I sit back in my chair again, but he's not buying the casual act.

"Yep, you do." He chuckles.

"Don't say anything about it in front of her, or anyone, okay?" I ask.

He pretends to zip his lips, but I have a feeling that's as permanent as a snowman in July. Oscar and Patricia stroll in, saying hi on the way, and after a minute, Lydia, Bev, and Sarah walk in together.

Sarah touches my shoulder. "Hey."

I sort of nod at her, conscious of Brent watching us with a Cheshire cat grin on his face. She pauses for a second, then takes her seat. When I finally meet her eyes, she looks hurt. Great. Exactly the opposite impression I wanted to give her after our date. I try to shake it off. Time for a redo.

Bev gets our attention. Sock watch, week four: socks again under the sandals this week. I'm starting to get the picture that when it's forty-five degrees or below, she wears socks. Above forty-five, no socks. Interesting.

"Let's do a check-in. Anyone have anything they'd like to share?"

Lydia raises her hand. "I've begun to have visions that I'll see Sister Mary Margaret again soon."

She crosses herself. Her face is paler than usual, I think, and her hand shakes.

Bev slides her therapist face on. "Tell us what you see."

Lydia blinks several times. "It's always before bed when I'm saying my prayers. Normally, Sister," she makes the cross, "would lie next to me and listen. I sometimes thought she was memorizing the holy Rosary, until I heard her snore." She smiles sadly. "Now, during vespers, I can feel her next to me. And when I open my eyes, she's there. It's happened too many times now to ignore. God is giving me a message." She pronounces the last part.

"What do you think the message could be?" Oscar's eyes are wide.

Lydia doesn't speak for a moment, and when she does, her voice trembles. "That He will send Sister to bring me to my heavenly home soon."

"Lydia," Bev says gently, "you aren't ill, are you? I don't think you need to worry about this—"

Lydia cuts her off with a sharp shake of her head. "It will be soon. I know it."

Bev closes her mouth.

"When my mother was dying," Patricia's voice is soft. "She said she saw my father several times. He'd passed a few years before. She said it was a comfort."

Lydia nods. "Seeing my Sister is, too." Cross.

"At least there's that," Bev says. "It sounds like this isn't upsetting so much as soothing, but please let me know if that changes. Thank you for sharing with us."

Brent raises his hand. "Ben has some news to tell the group."

I want to punch the smirk right off his face. Instead, I stare hard at him and stay quiet.

"No?" he asks. "Maybe I was wrong." He waggles his eyebrows at Sarah. "What about you?"

She stiffens, and her cheeks go pink. She doesn't look anywhere near me. "I don't know what you mean, Brent."

"My bad. I guess it was nothing." His voice is nonchalant. "Continue, Beverly."

Bev's confused gaze moves from Brent, to me, to Sarah, then to the rest of the group. Patricia and Oscar exchange glances. Lydia only looks distracted.

"Moving on," Bev says slowly, "the last few weeks we've talked about what we loved about our pets, how they made us feel, and our experience with grief or other negative emotions and how we handled them. This week, we'll discuss guilt. Guilt is an emotion that goes hand in hand with grief." Bev crosses her legs. "We might feel guilty because we don't feel we did enough for our pet. We might feel bad about how we handled other responsibilities while trying to cope with our pet's illness and death. We might also feel guilty about how we treated friends and family around the time of losing our pets." The therapist face comes out in force.

"Guilt is a sticky emotion, friends. It likes to stay around, and it can't be scrubbed away easily. I expect some emotion to come up today, and I urge you to accept it, welcome it, let yourself feel it. The next four groups, we'll be focusing less on the hard emotions and more on recovery, positive steps. So, take hope."

I swallow hard. Why did the topic have to be guilt today? You want guilt, Bev? I've got it in spades. Every week that goes by, and especially since my date with Sarah, I've felt increasingly crappy about keeping the truth about Bailey from her. But I'm pretty sure she'll never speak to me again. So—guilt.

I glance at Sarah. She looks worried. I smile, and she smiles back as if relieved.

"So, let's talk about it," Bev says. "Does the subject of guilt bring anything up for you?"

After a minute of silence, Oscar speaks. He usually smiles when he talks, but this time, his voice is low and he keeps his eyes down.

"I feel the guilt."

Bev waits patiently, but when he doesn't say anything else, she asks, "Can you tell us more about it, Oscar?"

He nods, then hangs his head. "I . . . killed my Baloney."

Lydia gasps and covers her mouth with her hanky. I'm a little shocked myself. Oscar nods.

"My Edith and me, we sometimes let the cats out in the backyard to take some sun. They weren't outside kind of cats, so we watched them close." He draws in a long breath, and the story comes out in a rush. "But one day, Edith was watching the *nietos* inside, and I was in a hurry to get the lawn mowed and the grass was very long and Baloney, he didn't hear too good anymore . . ."

Patricia leans away from him slightly with a horrified expression, and it's Sarah's turn to cover her mouth.

"Oh, Oscar. How awful for you," Bev says.

A few fat tears drip down Oscar's face. He doesn't wipe them away. "And for my Baloney. And Cheese saw it happen. It was my fault."

Patricia puts a hand on his arm. "Oscar, you didn't know he was there. Of course, you didn't mean to run him over with the lawn mower."

He shakes his head, looking surprised. "No, that's not what happened."

A quick glance around tells me everyone is as confused as me.

"But you said—" Bev starts.

"No, he saw or felt the mower or something and jumped at the last minute. But that was it for him. His heart gave out."

It's hard to say a heart attack is better than getting run over by a lawn mower, but after the scene we were all probably imagining, somehow it is. Patricia pats his arm.

"Oscar," Bev says. "We're all human, we make mistakes. And some of those mistakes have consequences that are so very difficult to live through. But you have a choice. You can condemn yourself or you can forgive yourself. You can choose to believe that you were responsible for Baloney's death or that your love and care for him over his lifetime more than made up for your small role in his passing. I want you to think about that, okay?"

Oscar nods and wipes his nose with the back of his sleeve.

"Thank you so much for sharing your story, Oscar. That was very brave." Bev looks to the rest of us. "Would anyone else like to share?"

We all eye Oscar, who's still quietly crying while Patricia offers him tissues and tries to comfort him. Hell no, we don't want to share.

"What about you, Ben?" Brent says. "What's your guilty story?"

I glare at him this time, and Bev clucks her tongue. "No one is obligated to speak in group, Brent. Please don't pressure him."

"It's kinda crappy though, isn't it? The rest of us tell the group stuff, and one person doesn't?" Brent's expression is affronted but behind it, I can tell he's messing with me.

"Ben might tell his story, and he might not. That's up to him," Bev says. "Anyone else?"

Brent's still staring, challenging.

"No," I say. "I will. Why not?"

As I say the words, the black hole of guilt in my stomach grows. I'm sweating now, too. This is a bad idea. I'm about to compound my lie with even more lies. Why did I fall for Brent's ridiculous I double-dare-you challenge? Too late. Everyone's looking at me.

"Um, when Bailey died, I . . . I wasn't really there for him." Because I was busy playing baseball and riding bikes with my friends. My parents took good care of Bailey as he got older and then got sick, but I can't say I did much other than hang out with him in front of the TV after dinner. I guess that was something.

There's concern and a little confusion in Sarah's eyes. Uh-oh. Did I say something that contradicted something else I'd told her? See, this is the trouble with lying. I'm bad at it. Can't keep my story straight. I shoot a dark look at Brent.

"I mean, don't get me wrong, I loved him. And it's not like he suffered or anything because I wasn't around . . . I don't think . . . but I wish I'd spent more time with him before he died."

All of that could be said to be true. All the splitting of dog hairs is giving me a headache.

Bev nods. "I can understand that. We're all busy, and sometimes, between work and other responsibilities, our pets don't get our full attention, even when they need it."

Sarah nods. I really wish I didn't see tears in her eyes.

"I could have spent more time with Sam, too," she says. "If only I didn't take so long at the grocery store or . . . or if I hadn't had to work so much. I could have taken shorter showers. And I slept in sometimes on my days off instead of waking up to be with him . . ."

Bev tilts her head. "Those all sound like things you had to do, Sarah. Not choices you made."

"But the extra-long showers . . ." Sarah wipes under her eyes carefully.

"Can be forgiven, I expect," Bev says. "Self-care is important when we're nursing loved ones—and when we're grieving."

Sarah smiles sympathetically at me, as if we shared a bonding moment. If I could shrink to about two inches tall, I would, because that's as big as I feel. Thanks to Brent, that butthead, I lied even more today, and Sarah bought it hook, line, and sinker. If she ever finds out, she'll never forgive me.

I suck. But I can't bring myself to ruin everything by telling the truth.

Chapter Eighteen

Sarah

As group ends, I'm still thinking about what Ben shared. We seem so similar, especially how we felt about our dogs. It's uncanny.

Bev rushes out of the room as usual, hurrying to her next commitment. But Ben, Brent, and Patricia stick around while I help Lydia gather up her things. She looks really fragile tonight, like a passing wind could blow her over.

"Why don't I walk you to your car?" I ask.

"Thank you, dear, but I'll be fine. Must be strong." She gives me a small smile, and I watch, worrying, as she totters out of the room to the elevator. I finally turn to the others.

"I hope it's okay that I invited Oscar," Patricia says to me. He still looks a little red-eyed, but at least he's smiling again. He has the sweetest smile.

"Of course," I say.

I don't mind Oscar coming, but the more people who know about the after-party, the more likely it's going to come to an abrupt end if Bev finds out. And honestly, I enjoy and get as much out of the casual conversations over coffee as I do the group itself.

I sit between Ben and Patricia at Alleycat. Ben seems preoccupied. He doesn't say much, but he does sneak peeks at my face as if to judge my mood or something. I try to smile at him every chance I get. Encouragement, I hope.

"Can I buy anyone a coffee?" Oscar asks.

Brent smiles smugly. "Black coffee—"

"And a muffin," the rest of us say tiredly.

"Thanks, bro," Brent says to Oscar.

Oscar looks confused by our response, but he doesn't ask.

I offer to buy Patricia's drink today, and this time she accepts. I also ask Ben, but he shakes his head.

"I'll go with you to order, though."

"Are you okay?" I ask as quietly as I can once we're in line. Oscar is in front of us.

"Yeah, only thinking. Hey, I wanted to tell you I had a great time on Sunday. Would you want to do it again? Not a dog walk this time. Maybe dinner."

Heat rushes from my chest to the top of my head. I was hoping he'd ask me out again. "I'd love to."

When we get back to the table, Patricia's speaking to Oscar and Brent's eating the muffin Oscar bought.

"Thanks for inviting me," Oscar says. "I didn't know you did this."

"It sort of came together over the last few groups." I think about telling him not to mention it in front of Bev, but then again, he's a grown man. I'm sure he doesn't need a reminder.

"Glad you could make it, Oscar. I didn't think I would get any more snacks out of the rest of them." Brent laughs while Oscar looks puzzled again.

"Have you called Travis, Brent?" I ask pointedly.

He squints. "Uh, no."

"Why not?"

"I haven't gotten around to it. What are you, my mother?"

My eyes narrow. "No, but I made a special effort to call him for you, and he might have done some research or made calls for you, too. It's rude not to follow up."

"Sorry if I'm being *rude*, but I've got other things to do."

Oscar and Patricia's heads swivel back and forth between us; they clearly don't know what we're talking about.

"Brent said he's interested in going to school to be a veterinary technician," I say, "so I called my own vet for him."

Their expressions show they understand now. Patricia says, "Sarah's right, Brent. You should follow up."

Oscar nods. "I got my job when a friend made a call for me."

"All right, all right, I'll call him this week." Brent puts his coffee cup deliberately to his mouth.

The subject changes to Oscar's four grandkids and how the oldest grandson's team won the city basketball championship last weekend. I also ask Patricia about Raymond.

"Did you talk to him about the dog thing?"

Her lips pinch. "I tried. But we got to fighting about my lipstick."

"Your . . . lipstick?" Ben asks.

She flings a hand in the air, her stacked bracelets falling down her forearm. "Ugh. He's so . . . aggravating. First, we had a discussion about why he says he doesn't want pets."

"Why doesn't he?" Ben asks.

She holds up three fingers. "Expensive, dirty, limiting. He said he got tired of the bills for medicine and special food for Snickers when she got older. And he hated when she pooped or peed in the house at the end, although he *knows* she couldn't help it. And he said he wants to travel more when we retire, and he thinks a dog will prevent that. As if we never boarded Snickers."

"Maybe you could pay for a new dog's expenses out of your salary," I say.

"That's a good idea," Patricia says.

"And take it to one of those trainers to be sure it's fully house-trained," Ben says.

"And you could trade with a friend, maybe, when you're out of town," Oscar suggests. "They watch your new dog, and you watch theirs." Ben and I nod in agreement.

"Yeah, yeah, but what about the lipstick?" Brent asks. "What was that about?"

"Well, we were in the middle of making up—"

Brent gets a sly expression. "Making up. Or making out?"

"None of your business," Patricia snaps. "But then, he tells me not to kiss him on the face because my lipstick doesn't come off easily and he's going out to dinner with his children!"

"Where did he want you to kiss him?" Brent asks.

"Brent, shut up," Ben says.

Brent pulls a face. "Make me."

"Don't be juvenile, Brent," I say.

"Don't be a bitch, Sarah," he says.

Ben shoots out of the bench on our side of the table and over to Brent, sticking a finger in his face. "Don't call her that."

The rest of us stare. I'm so shocked by Brent's name calling and Ben's reaction, I can't find any words for a minute. "Ben, it's okay. He's just being a jerk."

Ben shakes his head, still hovering over Brent. "I'm tired of him being a jerk. And you don't deserve to be called that when you've tried to help him."

Brent pushes Ben aside and stands. When he swings his backpack onto his back, I notice the bottom looks darker than the rest of the material, as if it's wet again. "I'm out of here. This was fun for a while, but I don't need people getting in my face. I've got enough problems." Head down, he storms out.

Ben sits in Brent's chair. He still looks furious, but he takes a long breath. "Sorry about that."

Oscar gently knocks him on the shoulder. "Brent shouldn't have called Sarah that."

I agree, but Ben's reaction surprised me. Brent was being vile, but Ben's reaction seemed a little out of proportion. Is something else bothering him?

"Maybe we should wrap this up," I say.

We walk back to the church making careful small talk. Ben and I wait, waving at Patricia and Oscar as they start their cars and leave.

"I'm sorry again, about earlier," Ben says.

I lick my lips. The dry night air plus the coffee has them feeling like sawdust. "Thank you for defending me, but . . . is anything else wrong?"

"No, why?" he asks quickly. A little too quickly.

I tug my curls out of my eyes to see him better. He looks so handsome, even in the dim parking lot lights, but there's a shadow of something in his face and posture. Something that looks a lot like guilt.

Surely, he's not thinking of Bailey still. But if not Bailey, then what?

Chapter Nineteen

Sarah

I check myself in the mirror one more time before I leave through my front door. Makeup and hair are on point. Ivory peep-toe heels, a slim cream skirt, my favorite silk blouse, and a scarf to pull the outfit together, plus a blazer. It might be spring, but it's still cool in Colorado in late April.

Rose answers the door when I ring, and my jaw falls open. I scoop up Miss P, who does her best to lick my makeup off, and take in my friend. She's wearing a leopard-print bodycon dress with a push-up bra, heels, and bright red lipstick. A leather jacket is slung casually over her shoulders.

"Rose . . . you look, I mean . . . wow. Amazing! But—where are we going?"

She smiles like the Mona Lisa. "Oh, Sarah bird, you'll see."

I groan to myself. I've been a bridesmaid enough times now to have a good idea. It's The Man Cave, Fort Collins's one and only male strip club.

Usually, I have to plan the bachelorette party, following the bride's requests. Which means I've dealt with The Man Cave more than once. This time, though, Rose did her own planning. She wanted it to be a surprise. I thought it might be dinner and drinks with her friends. Looks like I was sadly mistaken.

"Come on, Damon and the Lyft will be here in," she checks her phone, "thirty seconds." She puts Miss P inside and locks her door.

I had no idea Rose had ever taken a Lyft. Why I thought she wouldn't have taken one is probably pure ageism. Exactly thirty seconds later, a fancy silver Audi SUV pulls up and a handsome guy with jet-black hair and smooth, olive skin jumps out. He asks me, "Are you Rose . . . Bush?"

Rose smooths her sleekly styled gray hair. "That's me."

His eyes widen as he checks her out. "I'm Damon. Looks like we have some pickups before we get to our destination?"

"That's right."

He opens the door for us and helps Rose and then me into the back seat.

"Who's coming?" I ask. "Sylvia and Lucia?"

She nods. "We'll go for drinks and a light meal first, and then on to the main attraction."

I do my best not to sigh.

Sylvia and Lucia live in Charles's independent living community. They introduced the happy couple at a charity event two years ago. The women are waiting at the portico-covered front entrance, where Damon opens the car doors for them. They're dressed a little more conservatively than Rose, but not by much.

Sylvia, a tall, glamorous silver-haired woman with bright blue eyes and barely any wrinkles, sits with Rose and me in the back seat, and Lucia, a beautiful Latina with naturally black hair with only a few grays sits up front. Despite all my care in dressing, I somehow feel like the schlumpy, younger chaperone for this pride of lionesses.

"You ladies look lovely tonight," Damon says. "We're going to the Emporium, right?"

"Yes, with a stop at the Sunset Lounge first for drinks," Rose says.

"Great choice. Good cocktails." He glances in the rearview mirror. "What's the occasion?"

"I'm getting married," Rose says, "and this is my bachelorette party."

He grins. "Excellent. Sounds like you're in for a fun night."

I groan inwardly this time. Somehow, I doubt it.

At least the dinner and drinks should be quality, like Damon said. The Emporium and the Sunset Lounge are at the grand old Elizabeth Hotel downtown. And it only takes a few minutes to get there.

"Have a great time," Damon says as we pull up to the bellman out front.

"Thank you, Damon. We will." Rose winks at him, and he winks back. Odd. I have a bad feeling I might need a hand with these three before the night's over.

As we enter the lobby and head for the elevator, Sylvia stops us. "I have something for the bride-to-be." She digs in her purse and pulls out a pink sash which she unfolds with a flourish. We all laugh at what's printed across the fabric: He Put a Ring on It.

Sylvia hands out more folded pink sashes to Lucia and me. I hold my breath and hope for the best while simultaneously expecting the worst.

During previous duties as the MOH, I've had to wear male private parts on my head. Twice. Another time, I had to endure a T-shirt that said Maid of Dishonor all night. This time, it's the relatively tame Bride Tribe for the rest of us. The sash even compliments my outfit. I say a silent prayer of gratitude.

The host escorts us to a table in the corner of the lounge with beautiful views of town and the Front Range beyond. For a few more minutes anyway. The sun's disappearing beyond the tops of the peaks.

We order drinks from our waitress, a glass of chardonnay for me, which I plan to chase with at least two glasses of water to be on the safe side, and cosmopolitans all around for Rose and her friends. We chat about Sylvia's and Lucia's families and the upcoming wedding on Memorial Day weekend.

Ang's wedding is a few weeks before that, the first weekend in May. Her bachelorette party was a low-key sleepover that we held at her home, watching favorite romantic comedy movies, eating junk food, and playing a few drinking games with her sisters, Jayla and Kennedy, and some friends. She let me plan it, and she loved every minute of it.

I thought Rose might invite Andrea, her daughter-in-law, up from Denver for her bachelorette party, but if we're going to The Man Cave, I can definitely understand why she didn't. The thought of all those sweaty, gyrating bodies, and all that furry body hair, makes my head hurt. Yes, they're fantastically fit, but it's also fantastically mortifying.

"Sarah?" Lucia asks.

Oops, I missed something. "Pardon?"

"Who are you bringing to Rose's wedding?"

"Yes, we need an update on your love life," Sylvia says. "So we can live vicariously."

The threesome smiles at me expectantly. They've all been married before. Rose was widowed, and Sylvia and Lucia are divorced. I feel like the pathetic main character in a rom-com—the only one who hasn't managed to snag a man yet. Perennially the bridesmaid, never the bride. You know the one.

I'm tired of that story line. I want a new one. The words come out of my mouth before I think about them.

"I'm going to invite a new friend. A guy." I don't think I can call Ben my boyfriend yet.

Sylvia claps excitedly, and the women lean in. Lucia says, "Tell us all about him."

"Where did you meet him?" Sylvia asks.

I glance at Rose. I haven't had a chance to tell her about my date with Ben yet, but she saw me leave with him, so this can't be too much of a surprise.

"His name is Ben. Ben Becker."

"Good name. Strong," Sylvia says.

"And I met him at . . . a group I'm part of." I don't feel like getting into the pet grief support group thing. I hurry on. "We've been on one date already, and we're going on another this weekend."

"That's wonderful, Sarah bird," Rose says. "I'm so happy for you."

"What's stopping you from inviting him?" Lucia rejigs her sash over her glittery black top that perfectly shows off her curvy figure.

"Um, I don't know. It's still new, I guess."

"But the wedding's next month," Sylvia says. "You should ask him. He might make plans."

"That's true," Rose says.

Lucia puts a decisive hand on the table. "Call him."

"Yes, call him now," Sylvia says. "We want to be part of the romance."

I look at the women, eyes alight. I'm suddenly back at a middle school birthday party with my friends urging me to prank call my seventh-grade crush, Teddy Atkinson. And I feel about the same way—sick to my stomach.

"I don't know. He's probably busy right now."

In fact, I know he is. I'm missing the fifth Lost Paws group tonight. Rose and her friends have a variety of family plans over the next few weekends, so she planned her party for a Tuesday night. I've never been to a weekday bachelorette party, but then again, I've never been to a bachelorette party consisting of only seniors—and me.

The women look disappointed with me. I take a studied sip of wine. I can't believe I'm about to say this. "How about if I text him instead?"

Sylvia shakes her head at her friends. "These millennials. I feel so sorry for them. They aren't capable of an actual phone conversation."

"I'm shocked they go on in-person dates at all," Lucia agrees.

I try not to bristle. It's not like I haven't heard this before. My generation is probably the most maligned in history. Not that we don't deserve *some* of it, but c'mon, we're doing our best here. And it's not as though the boomers don't have their own problems. Such as blithely destroying the environment.

I pull out my phone. "Look, I'll do it right now. Happy?"

Sylvia claps again. "Can we watch?"

"Um, sure?" In for a penny, in for a pound. All eyes are on my thumbs as I type out a text.

Would you like to be my date for a couple of friends' weddings?

I text him the dates and sit back in my chair to wait.

"Good girl, Sarah bird. That was brave," Rose says.

Sweat pops up on my forehead, making me clammy. Fingers claw at my insides. I've only had half a glass of chardonnay. Shouldn't the drunk texting come later in the evening?

What if Ben says no? Or worse, what if he makes up some lame excuse for why he can't go? What if he thinks I'm a loser who can't find a date to a wedding or emotionally handle her dog dying?

What if—?

A text comes back. *I'd love to. Thanks for inviting me.*

Grinning, I hold out my phone to the table, and the ladies cheer. Sylvia hails our waitress. "Another round. We're celebrating over here!"

Great, I gave them an excuse to drink more. But I have to admit I'm floating on a rainbow as I send him a quick summary of the details of times and places for the weddings. Ben said yes! I finally have a plus-one!

There's still a niggling of doubt about his veracity, but the ladies were right. It was Do or Lie, er, die time.

We decide to order tapas in the lounge rather than a full meal at the restaurant downtown. As we eat, the others have a third round of cocktails.

Rose pays the check. She insists, ignoring our attempts to at least split it, and then looks at her watch. "Time to go."

I prepare myself mentally for the strobe lights, disco balls, loud electronic music, watered down drinks, sticky chairs, and screaming women.

"I need to use the ladies' room," Sylvia says. Lucia and Rose go with her.

"Text Damon, please," Rose calls to me, "and meet us in the lobby."

I do as I'm told. When Rose and the others come down, they don't have their coats on. And instead of walking to the door, Rose waves to me to follow her toward the meeting rooms that run along a back hallway. Sylvia and Lucia look as perplexed as I feel.

"Where are we going?" I ask when I catch up.

Rose pulls open a tall set of doors. "Here!"

It's the hotel ballroom. Inside, the heavy drapes are closed, but all the lights are on, and pop music is playing. Damon is there, stretching, wearing ballet tights and a muscle shirt.

Lucia moves to the music, her dark hair bouncing. "What's all this?"

Rose's eyes twinkle. "I love those wedding videos where the bride and bridesmaids do a coordinated dance together down the aisle. I thought we could learn one together. I hired Damon from the dance program at CSU to choreograph it and teach it to us tonight."

"Come on in ladies!" Damon says. "Kick off your shoes for now. We'll learn the moves barefoot, and then try it with heels. But first, some stretching to loosen you up."

"I'm already loose, let's get to the dancing!" Lucia shimmies across the floor toward him, making the rest of us laugh.

I'm no great dancer, but I'm so relieved, I could pee. Ben Becker agreed to be my date to my best friends' weddings, and we aren't going to The Man Cave. This is turning out to be a fantastic night. The best in a long time.

And I didn't even think about Sam once.

Chapter Twenty

Sarah

Lost Paws, Session Six

My eyes find Ben's chair first thing as I enter the basement meeting room of Most Glorious Blood of Christ. I've missed seeing him.

We weren't able to go on our date over the weekend. I was asked to cover a shift for an ill coworker on Friday, and on Saturday, I went with Rose on an emergency vet run for Miss P.

She ate at least ten fancy dark chocolate wedding favors wrapped in elaborate gold foil that Rose had bought for the wedding. So Rose, Miss P, the CSU veterinary school intern, and I had a long evening of activated charcoal and lots of gold-laced dog vomit. It turns out schnauzers aren't great at unwrapping candy.

I'd apologized to Ben several times for having to cancel, and he seemed to understand. But when I asked how last week's group went, he'd only said it was "tense."

I sit in the chair next to him because Brent's in mine.

"Hi, how are you?" I ask.

He eyes my cheek as if he might kiss it, but then seems to think better of it. Most of the group is here. "Okay. How are you?"

"Good." I study him. "You look a little frazzled. Are you okay?"

The whites of his eyes are pink, and his cheeks look a little hollow, like he hasn't slept or eaten well. "It's been a little bit of a rough week at work. And Brent's not helping."

Ben glances over at the other man who's sitting, legs outstretched, ankles crossed, and hands on his head, staring at the ceiling.

I set my bag down. "Did you guys have words again?"

"Not yet. But a few last week." He looks like he'd say more, but Bev stands and starts talking.

"Welcome back, everyone. I have some sad news. Lydia is in the hospital."

My gaze skids back to my usual side of the circle. Lydia isn't there. I hadn't even noticed before. I have a strange compulsion to cross myself, and I'm not even Catholic.

"What happened?" I ask. "Is she okay?"

"She's in the hospital. I think it's safe to say she's not okay," Brent says.

"You know what she meant," Ben says.

Bev holds up her hands in the sign of a T. "Time out, people. First, Lydia gave me permission to let you all know that she had a minor stroke over the weekend. Luckily, she was able to call the paramedics quickly, so she got treatment right away." She pauses.

Oscar makes a whistling noise. "Her vision was true. She almost did join Sister."

Brent snorts. "Dude, she's old. And half the time, I wondered if she was nuts."

Bev's eyes narrow. "Let's remember the rules, please. We

don't talk about group members who aren't here. And 'nuts' is not a way to describe a person."

"We talked about Sarah last week," Brent says.

I sit up straight. "Wait, what? What did you say?" I glance at Ben, and he looks pained.

"I'll tell you later," he whispers.

"I'll bet you will," Brent says.

Bev clears her throat. "There's something else I'd like to talk about before we go any farther. Is there anything you all want to tell me? Because I get the sense there's been some fraternization outside of group." She says this with a smile, but her eyes hold a suspicious glint.

We all look guilty—except for Brent—but no one says anything.

"No?" Bev raises an eyebrow. "I know we only have three sessions left, but the rules are in place for a reason. They're important for maintaining good boundaries while we're in session."

Patricia and Oscar still look guilty, Ben and Brent shoot daggers at each other. I'm finally starting to understand why those boundaries might be so important.

I raise my hand. "Bev? I heard you, and I understand the rules, but I have a request. Can we please go visit Lydia at the hospital? I hate to think of her there alone during group."

Lydia shared that she has no family to speak of in town. I wouldn't want to be in the hospital alone. No one should have to be.

Bev looks doubtful. "I don't know . . ."

Patricia says, "I'd like to go."

Oscar nods. "Me, too."

"So would I," Ben says.

Brent shrugs. "Whatever."

Bev tugs her Adorabelle T-shirt down as she thinks about it. No socks today. Ben told me he has an informal sock watch—so far, Bev has worn them four groups out of six.

"If everyone is willing, I suppose it would be all right. This isn't officially sanctioned by Lost Paws, by the way. But I'll join the group if this is how you choose to spend your meeting time."

Brent jumps up. "Field trip to see the crazy lady."

Bev turns on him, her eyes flashing with anger. "Brent, if you're going to persist in calling her unkind names, I'm going to ask you not to join us."

He rubs his chin. "Okay, okay. It was a joke."

"When a name has the power to hurt," Bev says, "it's no longer funny."

I stand. "I can drive if anyone wants a ride."

"I'll go with you," Ben says. Patricia and Oscar agree.

Brent gives me puppy dog eyes. "Can I ride with you, pretty please?"

"If you promise to be nice to us and to Lydia."

He makes the sign of the cross with a sardonic smile. "Scout's honor."

"I mean it, Brent," I say.

"So do I, Sarah," he says.

When Ben's hands flex, like they're considering wrapping themselves around Brent's neck, I think I've made a mistake.

Brent should really walk.

❦

After checking in with the nursing staff, Bev pokes her head into Lydia's room at Poudre Valley Hospital. The Cache la Poudre River runs through Fort Collins. It means something along the lines of "hide the powder," named that by French trappers who had to bury gunpowder after being trapped in a snowstorm.

Fort Collins has such an unspeakably exotic history.

Bev steps inside and talks to Lydia for a moment, then waves us in. Lydia lays in the bed, oxygen tubing running into her nostrils. Her arms, usually completely covered in heavy black material, are bare, and they seem thin and gray against the white sheets. She has such a forceful presence in group, even when she's quiet, that I didn't realize she was so physically fragile. She seems shocked to see us as we file in.

"You all came? To see me?" Her voice is weak.

Bev takes one hand, and I take the other.

"It was Sarah's idea," Ben says. Lydia squeezes my hand.

"How are you?" Patricia asks.

"A little better. Mustn't complain."

Oscar lays a battered candy bar on her bedside table. "In case you get hungry. Hospital food is—" He makes a face.

"Hey, Lydia. How's things?" Brent asks. For him, that's about as good as it gets.

"Thank you all for coming. This is very kind of you," Lydia says. "Very kind."

"We're so sorry you're here," I say. And I'm sorry I brought Brent at all.

About halfway here, I was regretting it. He kept burping and refused to roll down the window, and Ben looked so disgusted and annoyed that I thought he would take a swing at him from the passenger seat. If Oscar and Patricia hadn't been on either side of Brent, he might have.

"When are they springing you?" Ben asks.

"At first, they said I could go home tomorrow," Lydia says, "but then they decided to keep me to talk to a psychiatrist or psychologist or some such person." Her lips purse.

"Why?" Patricia asks.

Brent smirks. "Why do you think?"

"Shut up, Brent," Ben says.

"They were talking about me when they thought I was asleep," Lydia says. "They called me *hyper-religious*. I told them about my visions of joining Sister," she crosses herself, "and that when I was lying on the floor after the stroke, believing I was going to see the Lord finally, that Sister," she crosses herself, "came and laid next to me. She was with me." She nods, her eyes glassy. "She was."

I put a hand on her shoulder. "I'm sure she was, Lydia. She was a wonderful dog, it sounds like, and that's what good dogs do."

"Good cats, too," Oscar says.

"Not Sev," Brent says. "He'd as soon choke me as hang out next to me. But I didn't mind."

A memory of Sam sneaks in. I'd been doing yard work and stepped in a hole, spraining my ankle. I couldn't put weight on my foot and cried with the pain. Sam barked at the fence separating Rose's yard from mine for a couple of minutes, smart boy, but she wasn't home. He came and laid beside me, his head on my stomach, his big, dark eyes so sad, like he felt the sprain as well as I did. We stayed there together for a few minutes until the pain subsided a little and I'd been able to haul myself up to standing. Then, he'd sat right by my side the rest of the day while I laid on the couch, keeping my ankle elevated and wrapped.

Lydia needs a Sam right now. Someone to be on her side and look out for her. I ask her, "Is it okay if I talk to your nurse?"

"Of course, dear."

I head for the central nursing station. A pretty, dark-haired woman with a badge that says her name is Raziah looks up from her station.

"Hi, I'm a friend of Lydia's," I say. "Can I speak to her nurse, please?"

"That's me. How can I help?"

I speak quieter. "Lydia tells me her treatment team thinks she might have a psychological issue. I'm no medical professional, but I've been with Lydia every week for the past six weeks, and I don't think she does. She is very religious, and I think a bit superstitious as well, but not mentally ill."

While working at the public library in a medium-sized town, my fellow librarians and I have plenty of chances to interact with mentally ill people. Lydia doesn't seem to have the same challenges.

"She's older and probably a little lonely," I say. "She really misses her dog." I tell Raziah about Sister Mary Margaret.

She asks me some questions about Lydia, which I answer as well as I can, and then she thanks me for my input, and I go back to the room to find everyone laughing.

"What's going on?" I ask.

"We're telling stories about times our fur babies got into something they shouldn't," Bev says. "Belle ate a ficus once. Or at least part of it before we caught her."

"Baloney ate Cheese's poop out of the litter box sometimes," Oscar grimaces.

Patricia laughs. "Snickers got into a bag of crayons that Raymond's grandnephew left at our house. She pooped rainbows for days."

"Sister ate a whole bag of dog food I left out." Lydia's smile is tentative but genuine.

The list of things Sam ate but shouldn't have is long. I tell them about Miss P instead, since it's fresh in my mind.

"Sev ate rats," Brent says, before eyeing Ben. "What about your dog?"

Ben thinks about it. "Um, I think Bailey ate, uh, part of a kitchen sponge once." His face reddens.

Brent watches him. "Uh-huh."

"Brent." I point at the floor. "Your backpack is dripping again. What is in there?"

"Nothing," he mutters. "I'll be right back." He walks out of the room.

What is it with these guys? Brent's perpetually swampy backpack is one thing, but I'm really distracted by some of Ben's weird reactions.

Why does it feel like he's hiding something?

Chapter Twenty-One

Ben

Sarah drives us all back to the church, and I head home, but once I'm there, I pace around. I can't lie anymore. I have to get this off my chest. The guilt is killing me.

Finally, I text her at nine o'clock. *Can I come by?*

Sure. Is everything okay?

I need to talk to you. It won't take long.

A long pause this time. *Okay.*

The porchlight is on when I get to Sarah's house, so I ring the doorbell. Sarah answers in her pajamas and a robe. Her hair looks kind of wild, and I realize it's the first time I've seen her without makeup. Naturally, she's gorgeous.

I kiss her cheek. "Hey, I'm sorry it's late. Can I come in?"

She smiles hesitantly, but steps back. "I'm boiling water for tea. Would you like some?"

I was planning to launch into my explanation and apology, but the idea of getting a few more minutes with her before she kicks me out is appealing.

"Grab a seat on the couch. I'll be there in a minute," she says.

The television is on and showing some kind of nature documentary. They're talking about frogs in the Amazon. I think. Honestly, I'm so worried about what I'm about to do, it might have been about the rain forest instead of the frogs.

"Do you like chai?" Sarah says. "I have decaf."

"That's great." I'm not sure I've ever actually had chai tea, but it doesn't matter. I'm guessing I won't get to finish my cup.

"It was good to see Lydia today. I'm glad we went," she says from the kitchen. "I hope they'll let her go home tomorrow."

"Me, too. She's a nice lady. Maybe a little odd."

Sarah sighs. "Aren't we all?"

On the coffee table in front of me, a photo album is open. I lean forward to get a closer look. The pages it's open to are full of Sam. Sam running, Sam sleeping, Sam panting, his pink tongue hanging out. Sam sitting in a patch of wildflowers. Sam and Sarah snuggling. She sees me turning pages.

"I was feeling a little down when I got home," she says. "It always helps to get a Sam fix." She carries a tray over with two steaming mugs with tea bags in them. Honey, a little container of milk, and a spoon sit beside them. I thank her and take my mug.

"Do you think the group has helped you?" I ask.

Holding her mug, she leans back against a pillow. "Like I said at the after-party that day, it's really helped to be around other people who know what it's like. Some of the things Bev has told us made sense, too, and I've tried a few of the group's suggestions, like journaling and letting myself accept feeling sad. And—" She pauses and tucks hair behind her ear. "Honestly, it's helped the most to know that you're here and you get it. If you hadn't lost Bailey, too, I'd feel ridiculous being so maudlin in front of you."

I clench my teeth. I'd been ready to start my spiel, but then she added that last part. I try and try, but the words won't come.

I can't tell her.

"Yeah—I do get it." Inside my head, I'm throwing furniture.

You're weak, Ben. You really are a lying jerk, like Sarah's always thought.

"So, what did you want to talk about?" she asks gently.

I stare at my tea. It's now or never, coward.

"I wanted to . . . find out what the dress code is for your friends' weddings."

She blinks. "Really? That's why you came all the way over here?"

Relief, frustration, and self-loathing swirl around in my gut, making me sick. I cover by being extra-upbeat and jokey. "You might have noticed I'm a sharp dresser. I like to be prepared for big events."

She tilts her head. "I did notice that. Well, I think Ang's will be a little more casual. It's at the Pine Mountain Inn, and I'm guessing a lot of guys will be in sport coats without ties. Rose and Charles are getting married at the—"

I kiss her. Sitting there, watching her mouth move, was driving me crazy. I was listening, really, I could repeat back every word. But I had to feel her lips against mine again. At least once more.

Sarah freezes, but then she leans in. I scoot closer. "Sorry. I couldn't help it."

She smiles, her lips curving up seductively. "Is this why you really came over? Because you wanted to kiss me?"

I hesitate, but it only lasts a split-second. "You got me."

"You could've told me that." Her eyes sweep my face; she's still smiling.

"In my text? 'Hey, Sarah, can I come over and kiss you?'"

She shrugs. "At least it would have been the truth."

Ouch. And just like that the bubble of desire bursts. We kiss for a few more minutes, and don't get me wrong, it's amazing. But I feel like the lowest kind of lying loser.

When I leave a half hour later, I still haven't told her. She closes her door, I walk down the stairs, and I bang my head a few times on the top of my car. Not hard enough to do damage. Only enough to hurt.

As I climb behind the wheel, cursing myself three ways to Sunday, I notice the curtains on Sarah's duplex neighbor's windows flutter closed.

Chapter Twenty-Two

Sarah

Ang and Julian gambled, and they won. They wanted an outdoor wedding, but Colorado doesn't always have the best weather in May. It can be cold, gray, rainy, and even snowy.

To account for the possibility, the couple planned an outdoor wedding ceremony, with the reception inside. If it's warm enough, the exterior doors of the reception room can be opened, if not, closed. And if worse comes to worst with the weather, meaning snow or freezing temperatures, everyone can cram inside for the whole thing.

We watch the forecast anxiously, but the sun rises the morning of the wedding to preside over an unblemished azure sky. Temperature at I-do time is projected to be a downright balmy seventy degrees. You can't ask for much better than that in May.

Ang, her sisters, and I primp in the bride's room of the Pine Mountain Inn. Ang told me that by agreeing to be her MOH, I saved her from a sisterly knock-down-drag-out fight. Jayla and

Kennedy would have been more hurt to be the one not asked than they were when neither were asked, she said. I guess it makes a sort of sense.

I sigh as I apply the last of my makeup. "You are so lucky to get this weather, Ang. What's your secret?"

"I willed the sky into submission," my friend says matter-of-factly.

"She means it," Jayla says.

"Oh, I know," I say.

"Ang used to will us into submission, too," Kennedy adds.

"And it worked," Ang finishes.

She stands behind me to zip my peony-pink dress. I hold my breath and suck it in. Once the zipper ascends, I smile. I don't look half bad. Thank the fashion gods for full-body Spanx.

"You look beautiful, Sarah," Ang says. Her sisters agree. "With a little more blush and lipstick, you'll be ready for that hunk waiting for you at the reception."

"Hunk? What hunk?" Jayla asks as she slides her earrings in. Ang let us choose our own jewelry, bless her. At twenty-six, Jayla's next in age to Ang.

"He's not a hunk," I say.

"He most certainly is," Ang says. "I mean, I'm sure he is, from the way you've described him. But I don't know for sure since you haven't bothered to introduce him to Julian and me yet."

"You've been too busy with wedding and family stuff!" I say, not very distinctly, as I layer on lipstick. I'm going with a mauve color. It seems to play nicely with the dress but still pop against my pale skin.

"That's no excuse," Ang says. "But it's my wedding day, and I'm marrying the most fabulous man on earth, so I'll forgive you. This one time." She turns from the mirror and slips her heels on. Her dress from The Quick and the Wed is simply sensational. She positions a sparkling headband in her carefully arranged loose updo.

"And you look absolutely stunning, Mrs. Angela Perkins." I hug her carefully. "I am so ridiculously happy for you and Julian."

It's true. Ang went through some ups and downs with men before meeting Julian, but it's been all up since then.

"I'm getting married. Can you believe it?" She squeals and hugs each of us in turn, then checks the clock.

"Any minute now, Maggie will come storming in, worrying about the cleanliness of the cake plates or something, and I'll be headed down that aisle."

About thirty seconds later, that's exactly what happens, except Maggie's stressed about the cocktail napkins having come in contact with the oysters. Or something. I block her out and focus on being here in the moment with my friend and her sisters.

Twenty minutes later, we're outside gliding down the aisle in front of Ang with smiling, teary guests in foldable white chairs to either side. When I don't see Ben at first, my stomach clenches. He wouldn't stand me up. Would he?

But no, of course he wouldn't. He's right there on the bride's side to my left. I smile at him, and I'm gratified to see his gorgeous green-and-gold eyes widen as he takes me in.

Nothing could be more perfect. Except, you know, if I were the one wearing white. I'm starting to have a tiny sliver of hope that maybe, just maybe, I'll have my chance.

After the ceremony and about a thousand group photos later, I follow Ang, Julian, and both of their families inside, where the reception is well underway. A jazz band plays in one corner, and short lines form at the two open bars. The older folks sit at tables, nibbling on the food we chose—which looks scrumptious —and a few intrepid souls grace the dance floor.

When the singer spots the wedding party coming in, she

winds the band down. "Ladies and gentlemen, please welcome Mr. and Mrs. Julian and Angela Perkins!"

The wedding guests break out in applause, and one or two howl their approval. I grab a glass of white wine from the tray of a waiting waiter and take a celebratory sip. One best friend officially married, and one to go.

As I savor the taste of the wine, hands slide around my waist, and a welcome face appears beside mine.

"You look . . . incredible," Ben says. I turn as he's kissing my cheek, so he ends up kissing my mouth. Which is perfectly fine by me. I'm so distracted by how much I'm enjoying it, I practically spill my drink on his shoes. He jumps back.

"Sorry!" I say. "I promise this is my first one." I hold the glass far away from me before kissing him again. "Thank you so much for coming. I know you don't know anyone, but I'm really, really happy you're here."

He pulls me close. "I wouldn't want to be anywhere else. Seriously. I'm honored to be your escort." He holds out a hand. "Speaking of . . . would you care to dance?"

I hesitate. "As long as you don't expect *Dancing with the Stars*."

"We could do the funky chicken, and I wouldn't care," he says. "So long as I get to touch your feathers once in a while." He takes my hand and leads me to the floor, where Ang and Julian are already showing off their moves. They've practiced, and it shows.

Ben takes me in his arms, and we move together. We're surprisingly decent, especially considering our bodies haven't ever been quite this close before. My skin heats up quickly; I wish I could blame it on the physical activity.

Other couples join us on the dance floor, and it starts to get crowded. Ben and I are pressed even closer, which again, I don't exactly mind. During a break in the music, he kisses me, and as he pulls back, he accidentally bumps into another man. He turns to apologize and then grins.

"Hey, Pete!" Ben says. "How are you?"

The man, already sweating despite being jacket-less and with his tie loosened, pumps Ben's hand. "Great! Long time no see. We need to catch up."

"See you in a few?" Ben gestures to the tables where people sit with full plates, and Pete nods, then goes back to dancing with his partner.

"Old fraternity buddy," he tells me. "We play in a softball league together."

"Softball, huh? I can't hit my way out of a nightmare, even when the bad guys are closing in."

"Me either." Ben laughs. "They only keep me around because I'm good for a case of beer after games."

"Oh, that's different!" I bite my lip. Be brave, Sarah. "Is the league starting soon? Maybe I can watch you play."

"Actually, it is. And it's co-ed—you can play, too, if you'd like. I hope you will." He twirls me into his chest and holds me there for a second. My skin zings everywhere we touch. "I want to see as much of you as I can, Sarah Newsome."

"I'd like that, too. Very much."

We dance a while longer, and then go for a drink and some food. Maggie stands by one of the serving stations pumping hand sanitizer into confused guests' hands. But she outdid herself. The food is superlative as promised, and so beautifully presented, too. The wedding is turning out to be perfect.

I introduce Ben to Ang, Julian, and Ang's parents and grandparents. The band leader interrupts our chatting.

"Everyone, please gather for the cutting of the wedding cake."

Ang hadn't wanted any speeches by the best man or MOH at the reception. She said everyone who came to their wedding should already know them. They don't need introductions.

Did I mention she's my best friend for a reason?

Ben and I step into the semicircle of guests as Ang and Julian cut their slices and feed each other. I clap and shout as they kiss.

"There you are," Pete says from beside Ben. His date, a pretty Asian woman with a satiny sheet of black hair and wearing a stellar royal-blue dress, stands with him. "This is my girlfriend, Ming. She's a graduate student at CSU." Ben introduces me, and we all say hello.

"How do you know Julian and Angela?" Pete asks.

Ben nods at me. "Sarah is Ang's best friend."

"Ah, got it. Julian and I work together." He elbows Ben. "So, last time we played, you were a single man. When did you two meet?"

"In college," Ben says. "Sarah worked at the library on campus."

I add, "We met again in a group about six weeks ago."

"What group?" Ming asks politely.

I laugh. "I know how this sounds, believe me, but it's a pet grief support group. We both lost our dogs, and we needed a little help getting over it."

Ben winces as the words come out of my mouth.

Pete pulls a face. "Dog? You've never had a dog, have you, Ben?" He looks at me. "This guy was the most allergic SOB in the frat house. He sneezed and coughed if anyone came back with fur on their clothes after *visiting* their dog. Dude, if you had a dog, why didn't you ever bring it to our games? Everyone else does. It's a freaking dog circus out there most weekends."

Doesn't have a dog? I blink and look at Ben, whose smile is frozen on his face. He rubs his jaw, but he won't meet my eyes.

"What kind is it?" Pete asks him.

Ming, who's been watching Ben and me more closely than her date, pulls on his sleeve. "Pete, um, let's go get some cake."

He looks confused, but he must see something on her face that convinces him not to argue. "Okay . . . yeah . . . well, good to see you, Ben, and nice to meet you, Sarah."

I nod, but I can't think of a single thing to say in return. My brain is on fire, lit up with warning signals.

"I don't understand," I say. "Why was he so sure you didn't

have a dog? What about Bailey? Why didn't you bring him to games?"

Ben stares at the people behind me, his jaw clenched. He takes a breath, and his face is pained when he speaks. "Because he was right. I . . . didn't have a dog. Not recently."

My body trembles, and my hand shakes as it finds my mouth.

He lays his hands on my arms. "Sarah, I can explain."

I shake him off. "Explain what? That you've been lying again? That you never had a dog and everything about Bailey was made up?" I'm having trouble breathing and tears fill my eyes. "What . . . what were you even doing in the Lost Paws group?" A terrible thought occurs to me. "Is this some sick way you have of meeting women? By *preying* on them in support groups?"

Ben shakes his head hard. "Sarah, no. It's not like that."

He takes my hand, but I snatch it back and try very, very hard not to raise my voice. I don't want to make a scene. As it is, several people around us are listening while pretending not to.

"I should have known," I say. "I *did* know. Why did I ever think you'd changed?"

Ben's as pale as the table linens. "Being in the group was a stupid bet I agreed to with my brother. I didn't mean to—"

"A bet? That group—Lydia, Oscar, Patricia, and even Brent—they were all there in good faith. But you," I step away from him, "you were there because of a *bet*? I can't even imagine what kind of despicable human you must be."

Ben flinches. "Sarah, please listen to me . . ."

"Why? You'll only lie again. Please go. Go away and leave me alone. Find some other poor girl to lie through your teeth to. Maybe you can pick her up at the celebrating celibacy group. I hear it's on Saturday nights."

As Ben calls my name, pleading for me to listen, I rush away, practically spraining my ankle in my heels. I have to get out of here and find a quiet spot before I completely fall apart.

Why did I think this time would be different? Why did I think he would be different?

Ben is the King of Liars—then and now.

And me? I'm the sad, trusting, perpetually single MOH. Always the bridesmaid, never the bride. Not even worthy of the simple truth.

How very sad.

Chapter Twenty-Three

Sarah

"Rose, how much bad luck can one person have?" I sob, right before, well, sobbing some more. I've used up half a box of tissues already, with no sign of stopping.

I'm curled on my friend's couch, a mug of what used to be hot chamomile tea with plenty of milk and sugar on the coffee table. Miss P lies in the space that my rounded body creates, her expression mournful.

"Oh, Sarah bird, I'm so sorry," Rose says from her chair. She'd finished her own mug of tea ages ago.

"How could I do it? How could I trust him again? I knew he was a liar. Why didn't I listen to my instincts that he would be untruthful again and stay good and far away?"

She shakes her head. "We can't see the future or know others' hearts, love. All we can do is take people at their word."

"But I could see the future! I mean, I should have been able to. Once a liar, always a liar."

Rose clucks her tongue. "Not necessarily. Now, how did he explain himself?"

I sniff and rub my nose. "He said something about a bet with his brother, but . . . I didn't exactly give him the chance to."

"Why not?"

I sigh. "I was so embarrassed and upset, I just told him to leave. I didn't want to make any more of a fuss at Ang's reception. It was so beautiful and so perfect, and . . . and . . . I was so hopeful I might have the chance to walk down the aisle myself. In white this time!"

It's a few more minutes and another giant wad of tissues before I can speak again.

"Has he called you since then?" Rose asks when I calm down again.

I nod. "He's called, he's texted, he sent flowers, he's come by. He sounds really sorry, but he did last time, too. Liars hate being caught!" Rose doesn't answer, but she doesn't need to. I know I'm right. "I don't want to talk to him. What can he possibly say that would atone for joining a pet grief support group when you've never even owned a pet?"

Anger boils up through the hurt and humiliation. Who does he think he is? He didn't only lie to me, he lied to Bev and the group, too. Repeatedly. Without shame.

Every time I think I should give him a chance to defend his actions, like he so desperately wants to, I think of that. A group of people trusted him to be who he said he was. And he betrayed us.

"Sarah bird, that night he came over to your house late?"

I nod. I didn't know she'd seen him, but I'm not surprised.

"Now, I wasn't spying. I only wanted to see what he looked like." Rose sounds distressed.

"It's okay. I don't mind that you saw him. Now you can throw bags of dog poo at him when you see him around my house in the future."

She smiles a little sadly. My joke might have been funnier if I wasn't half-sobbing as I said it.

"After he left your house, he hit his head several times on the hood of his car. He seemed upset with himself. What happened?"

I wipe my nose. "He came over because he said he wanted to talk. Only . . . once he got here, he never really seemed to spit it out."

She taps her mug with a fingertip. "I wonder if he'd been trying to tell you the truth then?"

My mind replays the video of that night. He did seem weird and conflicted and . . . like he wanted to tell me something.

But he had his chances. Every day since we met in group. He's not getting another. I glance at my watch, but I've put it on upside down and can't read the time. I crane my neck to see the ticking clock on Rose's mantle.

"Oh, great. I'm going to be late for group." It's Tuesday night, and boy do I have a painful story to tell during check-in.

"You decided to go?" Rose asks.

"They deserve to know. I'm sure Ben won't show his Lie Boy face there, but in case they see him around town or something, they should know the truth about him."

I hug Rose and gather up the mountain of used tissues to throw in the kitchen trash. A quick look in the mirror behind the mantle clock tells me I'm a mess.

So what. It's a support group—and it's my turn to be supported.

Chapter Twenty-Four

Ben

Lost Paws, Session Seven

"Welcome to our second to last group, friends." Bev's voice is as chipper as ever. But tonight, for the first time, it grates on my nerves. "Does anyone have anything they'd like to share?"

Sarah's voice is painfully shaky when she says I do from her chair beside Brent, at the same time that, well, I do.

She whirls to see me lurking in the meeting room doorway. She looks awful. Her hair is wild, her eye makeup is smeared, and she's wearing pajamas with a jacket. Don't get me wrong, she's still beautiful, but I can tell she's had a rough time the last few days. Because of me.

I'm pretty sure I don't look any better. I definitely don't feel any better. I couldn't get up the energy to go to work today.

But I'm here because I want Sarah to hear me out. That's it. Let me tell her the truth.

I stare at her, putting as much raw pleading as I can in a look, and she stares back, anger and pain pouring from her eyes. I didn't think I could feel worse. I was wrong.

Bev throws us a puzzled look but doesn't speak.

"He can go first," Sarah says quietly. She moves to her spot next to Lydia and takes her hand. With everything that happened, and probably because I'm a terrible human being, I forgot to wonder how Lydia was doing.

I want to shove my own hands in my pockets, but the ancient sweatpants I'm wearing don't have them, so I cross my arms.

"I owe you all an apology," I start.

Sarah snorts. "That's an understatement."

Bev raises an eyebrow. "Sarah, please, let Ben speak."

She nods. "Fine. Speak, Ben. Like a dog. But you wouldn't know much about that, would you?"

"No," I agree. "I wouldn't." The group exchanges confused looks as I run a hand through my greasy hair. "Like I said, I owe you all an apology, because . . . I lied."

"I knew it!" Brent looks satisfied. "I could tell something wasn't right with him."

"Brent . . ." Bev gives him a warning look.

I hold up my hands. "No, he's right. When I joined the group, I didn't have a dog that died."

"Bailey's alive?" Oscar's expression is hopeful. Brent rolls his eyes and groans.

I smile a little. "No, Oscar, he died . . . about nineteen years ago. Bailey was my dog growing up. And pretty much everything I told you about him was true. It did really suck to lose him, but it was also a relief because I have bad pet allergies."

I glance at Sarah. She's listening, but I can't tell how she's taking the news.

Patricia speaks up. "I don't understand. Bailey was your family dog? Why didn't you tell us that?"

"Because I didn't think you'd believe that I was here grieving a dog that died twenty years ago."

"I would have," Oscar says.

"As would I," Lydia nods.

"Not me," Sarah says. "I was right about you all along." She raises a challenging eyebrow. "Tell them about the bet."

"The . . . bet?" Bev repeats.

I cover my face with my hands for a second. I'm not sure which part of my explanation makes me look worse.

"I lost a poker game to my brother a couple of months ago. I couldn't cover my bet, so I agreed to do whatever he told me to. I thought he'd make me wash his car for a year or do his taxes. Instead, as a joke, he told me to go to this group." I scratch my chin. "Actually, it was supposed to be the celibacy group, but I talked him into Lost Paws instead."

"You joined the group because you lost a bet?" Brent cracks up. "That's kind of awesome. I wish I had."

"Well I don't think it's awesome at all," Sarah says. "It's abominable. Ben pretended to be a pet lover, a dog owner, and an honest member of this group. He lied to all of us and especially to—"

She doesn't finish. The group still doesn't know that she and I had dated. Does that mean we were lying to them, too?

"I did. And I'm really sorry," I say. "I never meant for it to go this far. I was going to come to the group once and then drop out."

"Why did you stay?" Patricia asks.

I glance at Sarah.

"He was probably having a good laugh about us with his brother and his friends. Telling them what total losers we all are." Sarah mimics my voice.

I shake my head and start to deny it, but Brent interrupts.

"Nah, I know why. He stayed because he has a thing for Sarah."

Everyone's heads swivel from Brent to Sarah to me. I'm here to tell the truth, the whole truth, and nothing but the truth, right?

"Brent's not wrong," I admit. "Sarah and I knew each other

back in college. And . . . I really liked her—then and now. But it didn't work out."

"Because you lied then, too," she says.

"I didn't!" I throw up a frustrated hand. "I know I couldn't convince you of this six years ago, and I won't be able to now, but I never lied. I really *wasn't* with Alexa anymore. You just refused to believe me!"

"Hmm, I wonder why," Patricia says sarcastically.

Bev shakes her head and stands. "Obviously, there's a history here that's between Sarah and Ben, and I don't think it's the time or place to hash it out. Ben, is there anything else you'd like the group to know?"

I look at the ceiling, gathering my miserable thoughts. "I'm sorry for a few things. First, that I came at all. It wasn't right to take advantage of you all to cover a stupid bet. Second, I'm sorry I didn't come clean earlier with you all, and especially with you, Sarah. But, seriously, after the first group, I wanted to be here. I liked being with Sarah, it's true, but I enjoyed being part of the group, too. Maybe that makes me a sick person—"

Everyone nods.

I sigh. "And maybe I am. But I hope you all might accept my sincere apology." I look at Sarah and then Bev. "So . . . I guess I should go now?"

Bev shakes her sockless foot, thinking.

"That might be best, Ben," she says. "Thank you for your apology and for your explanation. It takes courage to be honest —no matter when you finally tell the truth."

I take a last glance around at the group. Patricia and Oscar wear sympathetic looks. Brent's sporting a huge eat-dog-poo smirk, and Lydia's praying—hopefully for my eternal soul.

Sarah won't look at me.

I wait, wishing she'd look up, but she's staring at her knitted fingers in her lap.

What was I expecting? A full pardon with welcoming arms?

Don't be dumb, Ben. You knew the way this would end all along.

A relationship with Sarah? Yeah, right. It's never going to happen now.

Chapter Twenty-Five

Sarah

The room is silent until Ben closes the door, and then everyone speaks at once.

Lydia clutches her cross. "Such a perfidious young man."

"I can't believe he lied to us like that," Patricia agrees.

Oscar looks sad. "I liked Ben."

"Dude's a prick," Brent says. "I knew it all along."

Bev tilts her head, listening to each of them. "I hear a lot of hurt and anger in the group. And I understand. I'm shocked by Ben's admission myself. But, I wonder, have any of the rest of you lied to the group?"

I wriggle in my chair. Patricia suddenly finds a stray thread to pull from the hem of her shirt, Oscar's leg bounces up and down a few times. And Brent . . . looks totally normal.

Bev goes on. "Because I have a feeling there's something no one told me. Like that you were indeed socializing outside of session?"

I raise my hand, my face scrunched. "Bev, that was my fault."

"How so?"

"I was sort of the organizer. I was talking to Ben after the second group, and we decided to get coffee, and then Brent joined us, and after that, it seemed silly to leave Patricia and Oscar out." I turned to Lydia. "We were going to invite you, too, Lydia, but then you had the stroke. It's so good to have you back, by the way."

She squeezes my hand as everyone murmurs agreement.

"Anyway, Ben and I called it the therapy group after-party."

Bev nods. "And what did you learn there?"

No one answers.

"About what?" Brent asks.

"Each other, the group. The rule itself."

"The rule seems stupid," Brent says.

"I don't know," Oscar says slowly. "The rule might be a good one. We were fraternizing, and now Ben got kicked out of the group."

"Because he lied, not because we, er, fraternized," I say.

He tilts his head. "Maybe, maybe not. If we hadn't gotten together outside of group, maybe he would have dropped out like he meant to at first."

I think about that. He could be right.

"I learned in after-group that Sarah is a good listener," Patricia says.

"I learned that Brent never has any money," Oscar says. Patricia and I laugh. Brent grins.

"Patricia is fun to talk to," I say. "And Oscar is always kind."

"I learned that the Lord provides," Lydia says. We all look at her. "He sent me to this group. And He showed me that there are still people who care." She pats my hand. "Maybe losing my Sister Mary Margaret didn't mean my life was over." She nods to herself.

I gasp. "Lydia, you didn't cross yourself!"

She automatically lifts her hand toward her chest, but, slowly, she lets it rest again in her lap. "I know my sainted girl is in the Lord's hands or curled up as close to Him as she can get."

"Well, I didn't learn much," Brent said. "This was kind of a waste of my Tuesday nights, actually."

I scoff. "Whatever, Brent. If it was such a waste of time, then why did you come to after-party every week?" He opens his mouth. "And don't say for the free coffee and muffins!" He closes it again. "Travis told me he plans to help you get into a veterinary tech school. Is that really a waste?"

He has the decency to look a little ashamed. "Well, except for that."

"Darn right. I think you like the group, Brent," I say. "And more than that, I think you like being with us."

I'm positive that something sarcastic and mean is coming out of his mouth. But instead, he shrugs. "Maybe."

I could have fallen out of my chair.

Bev stands and walks a bit up front. "You learned some things about each other that maybe you wouldn't have learned in our sessions. But can you also see how it gets complicated to have relationships outside of group?"

I'd forgotten about Liar, Liar, Pants on Fire for a minute. I sink in my chair. Did I really bring this heartache on myself by agreeing to have coffee with him the first time?

"What do we do about Ben?" Oscar asks.

"What about him?" Brent says. "He's gone."

"Yes, but he said he was sorry. And no matter why he joined the group, he was one of us."

"I think Sarah should decide," Lydia says. "It sounded as if he wronged her the most."

Everyone looks at me. Patricia and Oscar nod.

"I can't decide anything about him yet," I say. "It's too soon."

"All right," Bev says. "It will be Sarah's choice. I'll contact you this week to see if you'd like to invite him to the last group or not."

I can't imagine wanting to see him again, but I agree.

Bev tries to salvage her lesson for today—actions we can take to help ourselves move forward after the loss of a pet—and she has some good ideas. Fostering pets, volunteering for a shelter or other pet rescue organization, writing a letter to your pet, creating a memorial of some kind, or holding a ceremony.

"And when you're ready to open your heart again," Bev says, "there are always new pets in desperate need of homes."

Could I get a new dog? Not yet. The pain of losing Sam still feels fresh, and even fresher with the new heartache caused by Ben. It's ironic, really. I got Sam soon after Ben lied the first time, and I lost him right before Ben lied again. There's something about the two of them . . . They're tied together in some way I can't quite put my finger on.

As Bev wraps up at the end of the hour, I raise my hand. "Since we already completely flouted the rules, can we have one more after-party at Alleycat tonight? And of course, you and Lydia are welcome."

Bev sounds tired when she answers. "I suppose you might as well. I can't join you but thank you for the invitation."

"What about you, Lydia? We'd love to have you."

"Oh, why not," she says. "The Lord can wait a little longer for his prayers tonight."

I pat her shoulder. It eases my bruised heart to know I don't have to go home to my empty duplex without Sam or even any coffee. I'm feeling a little better until I spot Ben waiting in the parking lot.

Patricia raises an eyebrow and mutters to me, "He waited out here all this time? That's devotion."

"That's guilt," I say firmly. "Go home, Ben." I shoo him with the hand not holding Lydia's arm.

"Sarah, I need to talk to you alone. Please." He shivers in the cold.

"No. Not tonight."

Brent swaggers to my side. "You heard her. Move along."

"Ugh, that's not helping," I say.

With a scowl at Brent and a last, tortured gaze at me, Ben gets in his car.

"C'mon everybody," I say.

"He does seem really sorry," Oscar says.

"And like he isn't going to give up easily," Patricia says.

"And like he needs a shower," Brent says.

For once, Brent and I agree.

The five of us settle into the Alleycat at our usual six-person table. I try not to think about the missing person. Before anyone can offer to get anyone else a coffee, I say, "Brent's buying."

He drops his backpack. "Oscar was right. No cash."

"Brent, everyone has bought you a drink and a muffin every week. It's your turn."

"No can do."

With a frustrated groan, I stand to go pay myself, but Lydia clutches my arm and presses a wad of cash in my hand. "If there's one thing the Lord has certainly provided, it's money. Please get me a cup of tea."

I smile and peck her hollow cheek. "Thanks, Lydia."

Oscar comes with me to get everyone's orders and carry them back to the table. He fiddles with his phone as we wait.

"I'm sorry about Ben," he says.

"Thanks, Oscar."

"I know it isn't my business, but I don't think he's a liar. He just didn't tell the truth."

I lean against the counter. "Isn't that the same thing?"

"Maybe. It depends on why he lied. He said he did it because he liked you, and he wanted to spend more time with you."

"Yes, but he should have told me the truth a long time ago."

"That's true. But he has now. So—what will you do?"

I exhale. "I don't know. We have a history, Ben and me. I already had problems trusting him, and this makes everything worse."

"I get it. It's like the first time I let Baloney into my room, and he pooped in my shoes. I didn't let him in again for a long time. Then, when I did, he acted like the perfect gentleman, you know? But I found out he was pooping in Edith's shoes!"

I wait, but he doesn't say anything else. "So, then what happened?"

Oscar takes one of the trays the nose-ringed woman behind the counter passes to us. "Nothing. We locked him out for good after that."

I'm not sure what I was supposed to learn from that story, other than not to borrow Oscar or Edith's shoes, but he's a good guy. I'm going to miss him when group is over. I chew on that thought as I grab the other tray and we walk back to the table.

"Hey," I say. "What do you all think about meeting here once a month after group finishes? That way we won't lose touch, and we can keep supporting each other."

Patricia puts her mug down. "Count me in. With the trouble between Raymond and me lately, I've spent way too much time thinking about him and Snickerpoodle and feeling sorry for myself."

"Can I bring Edith?" Oscar says. "She wanted me to be in the Lost Paws group, but now I think she's kind of jealous about the time I spend with you all."

"Of course!" I say. "What about you, Lydia?"

"If it doesn't interfere too often with my vespers, I will come," she says.

I hug her thin shoulders. "We'll make sure it doesn't." With an internal sigh, I say, "Brent?"

He shrugs. "We'll see."

Patricia rolls her eyes. "Don't let us cramp your style."

He winks at her. "I won't. In fact, I've gotta go. Hot date."

"Really?" It's hard to imagine anyone dating Brent. "I mean, have fun. Where are you going?"

"The haunted house out on Dayton—Ten Thousand Screams."

"But it's May." Oscar looks confused.

"It's a year-round one. For the true haunted house fan." He

slings his backpack on his back and shoves the last bite of muffin in his mouth. "See you next week."

We watch him go.

"That young man has dark spirits following him," Lydia says.

"Hopefully, he leaves them at the haunted house," I respond.

Oscar collects up Brent's empty mug and muffin plate and puts them on a tray. "Maybe he'll leave the dead *ratas* there, too."

I freeze with my mug halfway up to my mouth. "What?"

"Brent has rats in his backpack. The zipper was open, and I saw them."

"That's disgusting," Patricia says. "What do you think he's doing with them?"

My eyes widen as a thought occurs to me. "Oh, no."

"What, dear?" Lydia looks concerned.

I bite my lip and think before I answer. "Nothing. It's nothing."

I hope.

❧

I lie on my couch a few days later, wishing Sam were here to talk to. He would have sat on the other end of the couch, facing me, his black eyes patient and understanding, as I told him my latest crisis. Then, when I had talked myself out, he'd share a few licks of Chunky Monkey from my spoon. Chocolate bits removed, of course.

Normally I'd call Ang for advice, but she's on her honeymoon. No way I'll interrupt that to talk about pilfered rats and dead snakes.

I also secretly wish I could talk to Ben. I think he would understand the pickle I'm in. And he really is a good listener.

Here's the thing. In my soft-hearted stupidity, I vouched for Brent and asked Travis to support him. Travis agreed, including finding ways to help him financially. Now, I suspect that Brent is still stealing those rats, and possibly money, too, from the pet store where he works.

I think I have to tell Travis. I can't let him give Brent money if Brent's actively breaking the law. He might con Travis, or he might go back to jail and have to drop out of school and waste Travis's time.

I decide to call Bev. She'd left me a message earlier anyway.

She picks up after a few rings, and I hear a small dog barking in the background. My heart aches again as my eyes find the empty side of the couch.

"Bev, I want to apologize again for breaking your rules. I feel bad, and believe me, I'm pretty sure I've learned why it's better to keep personal relationships out of the equation."

She doesn't speak right away. When she does, she says, "Relationships formed in therapy or support groups can be intense. Getting involved with someone you meet there can lead to a wonderful relationship full of mutual respect and deeper understanding than someone you meet elsewhere . . . or they can be disastrous."

"Chalk Ben and me up in the latter category," I say. "Anyway, I'm okay with him coming to the last group."

"Are you sure?"

I tell her I am. I don't want to see Ben, but this isn't only about me. Other people were affected. I can be the bigger person and spend one more hour in the same room with Mr. Lying by the Seat of His Pants.

"I need to talk to you about something else, too, though," I say. "A problem has come up with Brent." I explain the situation.

"I see," Bev says. "I have some ideas of what we might do, but I'd like to hear your thoughts, first."

I tell her my plan.

"All right," she says. "I'll support you if you'd like to bring this up on Tuesday."

We chat a bit more about the details, and then we hang up. I only hope I'm doing the right thing.

I mentally smack myself in the head. What had I been thinking offering to connect Brent with Travis? He's a criminal, after all, even if stealing rats and some petty cash isn't exactly maximum-security type stuff.

I guess I'd done it because I believe everyone deserves a second chance. Something about that thought jangles in my brain, but I'm too exhausted and sad to suss out any meaning.

Chapter Twenty-Six

Ben
Lost Paws, Session Eight

I smell Sarah come into the room behind me before I see her; she wears a flowery perfume that I know instantly when I smell it now. I try to speak to her as she goes by, but she pretends not to hear me.

Everyone else is already here. Oscar spoke to me, seeming glad I was here, but the others only smiled a little or waved. Lydia shook her head sadly in my direction.

Bev called a few days ago and invited me to the last group. She wouldn't say much, but I hope this is a good sign Sarah might forgive me. Maybe. Not that I deserve it. I chew on my thumbnail.

After her welcome, Bev turns to me with her therapy face in full force. "As you know, Ben, the group agreed to invite you back today. And you are welcome. You might hear how your behavior affected other members of the group today, but I will ask everyone to share their feelings without attacking you." She sweeps the circle with her gaze, ending on Sarah, who nods.

"Thanks for giving me another chance to join you all," I say. "I am really very sorry for the mess I've made."

Bev continues. "Before we get into that in more depth, there's another issue we need to discuss. Sarah?"

Sarah turns to Brent with a concerned expression. He's been picking at the edge of the sole of his faded, torn sneaker, one shin crossed over the other knee.

"Brent," she says, "over the last few weeks, we've all noticed your backpack has often been wet when you come to group. Then, last week, someone," her eyes dart toward Oscar, "said they saw a package of frozen rats in there." She pauses. "I have to ask you: are you stealing them again?"

"No way, I pay for them." Brent shakes his head vehemently, but even I can see the truth all over his face. I stare. *That's* why his backpack's been dripping all these weeks?

"You're on probation," Sarah says. "You can get in big trouble for this."

He hesitates, then slides down in his chair. "Not if no one else knows."

Bev pulls her chair closer to him. "We can't merely ignore this, Brent. And I think you know that."

"Are you stealing money, too?" Sarah asks.

He crosses his arms and doesn't look up.

"Oh, Brent, you seemed to be doing so well," Sarah says. "Why did you start stealing again?"

He shrugs and doesn't say anything for a long time. "Having the rats in my freezer . . . it kept Sev closer."

Sarah nods, looking a little less upset. She probably can't say she's been stealing value bags of Purina or anything, but there's a reason she has pictures of Sam plastered all over her house.

"Brent," Bev's voice softens, "you need to tell your employer and pay them back for what you've taken."

"You're a therapist. You can't tell the cops what I say unless I'm going to hurt someone or whatever."

"I can," Oscar says.

Brent narrows his eyes. "You'd better not."

Oscar snorts at the implied threat. "If you don't, I will."

"And I'll go with him," Patricia says.

"And me," I add quietly.

Brent jumps up. "Fine. They'll send me back to jail for embezzling, but who cares, right?"

Sarah holds up her hands. "Brent, wait. Maybe we can work this out. How many rats have you stolen?"

"Dozens."

"How big is his freezer?" Patricia mutters.

"And how much do you think they cost all together?" Sarah asks.

"A couple hundred bucks. They're fifty dollars for a package of ten." He reaches in his backpack and pulls out a dripping bag with a green label that says Gourmet Rodent. The silhouette of a rat is followed by the size: medium. I can't see any actual rodents through the opaque plastic.

Lydia crosses herself. "Poor little things."

"Okay," Sarah says, "here's the deal. I'll lend you the money to pay your employer back with the condition that you'll write and sign a confession that I'll keep. If you pay me back in the next, say, three months, we forget about this. If you don't, I give your confession to the police and let them handle it."

He nods, looking relieved. "Yeah, definitely, that'll work."

"You have to write the confession before we leave today," she says.

"All right, all right. Give it a rest."

"Brent!" Sarah looks exasperated.

He holds up his hands. "I will. Promise." He sounds sincere—for once.

Bev stands. "Good. Now that that's settled, I want to leave the rest of the group to talk about how you all feel about your experience in group. What have you accomplished? What work is left to do? What did you get from the group, and what could have been better? And of course, if someone has something to say to Ben, now is the time."

I glance at Sarah, but she keeps her eyes on Bev.

Patricia raises her hand. "I have news. Raymond and I made up."

Sarah's face brightens. "What happened?"

"Well, he asked if we could have dinner and talk things over, and I said yes. He told me to dress nice, so I wore my sexy, low-cut burgundy lace dress and my highest heels, and—"

Brent groans and makes a hurry-up circle with his hand. "Spare us."

Patricia rolls her eyes. "Anyway, he took me to Frasca in Boulder. We talked for hours over dinner, and then, he gave me this and asked if he could move back into our bedroom." She holds out her right hand. A gold and diamond bracelet hangs delicately from her wrist.

"Beautiful!" Sarah says.

"That's wonderful, Patricia, but . . . what did you two decide to do about future pets?" Bev asks.

Patricia smooths her skirt. "Well now, we talked about that for a very long time. It seems it's not that Raymond doesn't like pets, it's that he felt—" She puts her fingertips on her temples. "This is going to sound so childish, but he felt that I loved Snick-erdoodle more than I loved him. He said I would greet her first when I came in from work, I snuggled with her more, and I was more concerned that she was being fed or walked than if he was being cared for. Especially after she got sick, Raymond felt left out."

Oscar nods enthusiastically. "Sometimes Edith said that about Baloney and me, too."

Patricia goes on. "We agreed that when we get another pet, we'll choose it together and do things like feeding, walking, or snuggling with it equally. And I agreed that I would pay more attention to him once we have it, although honestly," Patricia scoffs, "Raymond is a grown man. Snickers was my baby, and she needed me. But . . ." She holds up her hands and shakes her head, "I agreed to it all."

"That sounds like an excellent compromise," Bev says.

Patricia gets an impish expression. "And after that, we had a very romantic evening."

Brent shoves his fingers in his ears. "No one wants to hear about old-people sex!"

Patricia laughs. "You should listen and learn, son."

When Bev asks if anyone else has something to say, Lydia raises a hand.

"The Lord told me it was time to welcome a new pet into my heart." She nods. "I prayed on this for many a night since I was hospitalized, and I know that is what He wants for me. Although, after my stroke, I realized that a Saint Bernard like Sister and Brother might be too much for me now. So, I went to the shelter and asked Him to send me the right companion. I'd like you to meet Sister Lucy Helena." She holds up her phone to show a black-and-white cat hiding under a table. The feline's eyes are demon-red from the flash, but I'm sure she's cute. "Saint Lucy was said to be a bearer of light in the darkness of winter."

Sarah hugs Lydia, which makes me, somehow, jealous. To be honest, I'm shocked that Lydia is the first in the group to adopt a new pet. No one else seems to be in much of a hurry.

"That's wonderful news, Lydia," Bev says. "Sister Lucy is a very lucky cat."

"How did you know that God told you to choose that cat out of all the others?" Oscar's eyes are wide.

"Because of this." Lydia points to the cat's chest, where black fur on the white background creates a vaguely X-like spot. We all lean forward to study the picture.

"What . . . is it?" I ask.

"A cross!" Lydia's triumphant smile illuminates her wrinkled face. "I told you all in the first group, didn't I?"

"Told us what?" Patricia asks kindly.

"That the Lord would provide. He provided me with Sister Lucy Helena to comfort me after losing Sister Mary Margaret, just as he did after Brother. I only needed to have faith."

Lydia nods and slides her phone in her bag with a thump, as if to say, And that settles that.

Oscar speaks. "I have some news, too. I let Mustard sit on my lap while I watched the Rockies game, like I used to let Baloney. She's softer than he was, and she doesn't scratch up my legs." He says this thoughtfully. "But Baloney was still the best cat."

"I'm so glad you're finding space for Mustard in your heart, Oscar." Bev looks around the group. "What about you, Brent?"

"Huh?" He's sneaking a peek at his phone. "What about me?"

"You don't have to contribute, of course, but I'm wondering if you've learned anything in group."

"Yeah. I've learned not to keep my rats in my backpack. Makes a mess and people can't keep their eyes to themselves."

"That's it?" I say.

"Yep."

I shake my head and take a long breath, about to speak, but Sarah beats me to it.

"I learned something, too."

I brace myself. Here it comes, all the blame and condemnation that I deserve.

"I'll always love Sam. He was my whole heart. But being here with you all helped to show me something." She pats her chest. "I might have relied a little too much on Sam to fill the empty places in my heart. Places that probably should have been filled with people instead of a dog, no matter how great that dog was." She looks around, stopping short of me. "You all taught me that I'm not alone. There are others who loved their animals as thoroughly as I did. And we can all go on together, supporting each other, until maybe one day I'll feel like Lydia and know my heart is ready to be filled again. I'm not there yet, but I can see a very small glow at the end of the tunnel now, thanks to you."

"What a wonderful testament to the power of group healing, Sarah," Bev says. Sarah nods, her eyes a little wet.

Wow. She didn't yell at me, blame me, or condemn me. Yet. I unclench my jaw. Gotta make this good.

"I have something to say, Bev." I glance around the group. "Listen, I know I shouldn't have been here at all. That I really screwed up and broke your trust. But I want you guys to know that even though I haven't lost a pet in a long time, I gained something anyway from being here." I lean my forearms on my knees. "It's been a long time since I was part of a group of people not at all like me. At work, everyone's an engineer, a professional, or at least college educated. My friends are a lot like me, too. But here, everyone was different. I learned that I can hang out with a group of people who I didn't think I'd have anything in common with and find ways we're alike anyhow. I hope that despite everything I've done, I can call you all friends."

Oscar, Patricia, and Lydia nod. I don't dare look at Sarah.

"That's lovely, Ben," Bev says.

I hold up a finger. "Sorry, I wasn't quite done. I also learned, being here, that I wasn't over a certain girl I met in college. Not by a long shot. This girl is smarter, kinder, more caring, and even more beautiful than I remember. And . . . I really want a second chance with her."

Everyone's heads swivel from me to Sarah, and back to me, and back to Sarah.

"Don't you mean a third chance?" Sarah says. "If I give you another chance, it will be your third. Your second chance was when you lied to all of us for weeks about why you were in the group."

My chin dips to my chest. "I don't know how else to express how sorry I am about that. Please, Sarah, believe me."

Sarah's flat expression, the tense set of her shoulders, her crossed arms, they tell me everything I need to know. "See, that's the problem. I don't think I can anymore. Especially not now."

The others are silent.

After a minute, Brent sighs and slaps my back. "Give it up, bro. You blew it. It's over."

My heart withers in my chest. Brent, I'm afraid, couldn't be more right.

Chapter Twenty-Seven

Sarah

"Oh, Ang, you have no idea how great it is to have you back."

I fly into my friend's arms when she opens the door of her downtown bungalow. It's Sunday afternoon. Ang and Julian got back from their paradisal honeymoon in the middle of the Indian Ocean yesterday morning.

"How was Mauritius? Was the resort amazing? I got your texted pictures and saw your Instagram, but I know you have more, and I want to see every single one. Well, maybe not *every* one. I don't know what you and Julian got up to after all. And—"

I pause to stare around the living room. "Oh my gosh, what happened here? Did wedding fairies attack the house?"

Every inch of space is covered by wrapped wedding gifts, unwrapped wedding gifts, suitcases in various stages of being unpacked, open garment bags, and undistributed wedding favors.

She sighs. "Basically. Now you see why I invited you over."

I raise an eyebrow. "I'm glad you missed me."

She grabs my hand. "No, that didn't sound right! I also want to know everything that's been going on since the wedding. But first, what can I get you to drink?"

"White wine, please. Or red. Or tequila, scotch, whiskey, bourbon, or brandy. Whatever you've got. But make it leaded."

She eyes me dubiously, and then walks to the kitchen. She pulls out a bottle of white from the fridge and two stems from the cabinet. "O-kay. I can see we've got some talking to do while we work."

"You have no idea." I swing an arm at the living room. "Where should I start?"

"How about opening presents?"

There are several neat piles of gifts that Ang and Julian's families hauled over after the happy couple left the reception. "Ooh, the good part. But don't you and Julian want to do that together?"

"He has a huge project starting tomorrow at work. I don't think he'll have time to open them with me. Anyway, you and I will appreciate the gifts more than he will. Could you keep the cards or tags with the gifts, so we'll know who to thank?"

"Sure, but what are you going to do?"

"I'll unpack and start the laundry. I also need to sort our wedding clothes to return Julian and his groomsmen's tuxes to the store and get my dress to the dry cleaner." She hands me a very full wine glass.

I take a large gulp and shake my head. "I'll do that. You open your gifts. Just be sure to show me everything."

"All right then, I'll start with yours." She sifts through the piles until she finds the gift I'd wrapped in a matte silver paper with a big white bow. She slides a manicured fingernail along the seam and unwraps it.

"Sarah! You didn't. Oh. Oh—" Her agate eyes fill with tears as she studies the copy of *Annie Allen* by Gwendolyn Brooks. "This is unbelievable."

"It's not a first edition, but she signed it here, on the title page." I open the front cover gently and point at the poet's signature, dated 1989, to someone named Greg Gatenby.

"Julian and I will cherish this." Ang hugs me.

"I'm so glad you like it." I clutch her as emotion suddenly spins up from somewhere around my belly button. "You guys are so lucky. I'm . . . I'm so happy for you." And here come the tears. I swore I wouldn't cry today, too.

She pulls me into her shoulder. "Sarah, what is it?"

"Ben."

She rubs my back. "Tell me about it. C'mon, sit here." She leads me to the small rectangle of space on the couch that isn't covered in wedding detritus.

"But we have . . . so much to . . . do." I gesture to the piles as I sob.

"It can wait. What happened?"

I tell her—in halting sentences punctuated by hiccups, tears, and a few not-so-nice names—what happened at their reception and at the last Lost Paws group. She holds my hand and listens intently.

"So, where do things stand now?" she asks.

"Nowhere. I told him I never wanted to see him again. Except . . . I invited him to come back for that last group."

"Why?"

"Because I didn't want to be the one who said he couldn't come."

"And did you talk to him then?"

"Only to tell him, again, that I've given him enough chances to lie to me."

Ang nods, her expression thoughtful. "But he didn't lie only to you, did he? He lied to everyone."

"I know!" I pat my face with a tissue from my pocket. I've taken to carrying the little plastic packs with me at all times. "Isn't that awful?"

"Yes, it was."

I glance at her. She doesn't exactly sound outraged. "What? You don't think it's bad?"

"I didn't say that. I just, I don't know if I think it's as bad as you seem to think it is. Was anyone in the group hurt by having him there?"

I run a fingertip along my glass. "I mean, other than feeling kind of used, maybe—no. Not that I heard."

"Then, did it really do that much harm?"

Bristling, I face her. How does she not understand? "That's not the point. He lied again. Like he lied in college. And when was he going to admit all this? If that frat brother of his hadn't busted him at your wedding, I might have gone along happily dating him—when he's never even loved a dog!"

"Inconceivable," Ang says wryly.

I sigh. "Ang, I know dating an animal lover wouldn't be high on your list of priorities, but it is on mine."

"Oh, trust me, I know. But listen, Ben didn't say he didn't love dogs. He's allergic to them, right?"

I nod.

"And he liked you enough to take you to a pet charity event and sit through a group of people talking about how much they missed their pets for eight weeks, didn't he? Eight weeks, Sarah." She smooths my collar down, like my mom might have when I was a girl. Her voice gentles. "Plus, you've seemed happier since you met Ben. Less sad about Sam. It might be the group, of course . . . but it might be him."

I have to agree that's true. The hole in my heart isn't as raw these days. "So, you think I'm overreacting to this?"

With a sympathetic expression, she holds up two fingers, one a short distance above the other.

I think about that as Ang sits quietly by. "But, if I give Ben another chance, how will I ever trust him?"

"He said he didn't lie back in college, right? Did you have proof he did?"

I snort. "The text from Alexa seemed pretty incontrovertible."

"But other than that?"

I mess with a stray thread on my jeans. "No. That was it. He insisted what Alexa said wasn't true . . . Only, I mean, I read it myself."

"You believed some woman you'd never met instead of Ben, who up until then had been trustworthy?"

I squint. "I never thought about it that way."

"And although it took him too long to tell you all the truth about how he joined the group," she says, "I can at least tell you *why* he lied."

I blink. "Why?"

"Because, beloved-but-dense friend, he didn't want to blow another chance with *you*." She shrugs. "If it were me? I'd give the boy another shot. But it's not me, it's you. Do you think you can forgive him?"

My eyes sweep the room filled with tangible expressions of family and friends' love for Ang and Julian, and the couple's love for each other. I want this so badly for myself someday.

But there are plenty of dogs in the shelter.

Do I want it enough to open my bruised and broken heart to that mutt Ben again?

Chapter Twenty-Eight

Sarah

Unlike Ang and Julian, Rose and Charles must have angered the weather gods.

I wake up to rain and mist the morning of their wedding. I have to scrounge around for an umbrella to get home after my hair styling and manicure appointment, and by the time Rose and I leave for the chapel, it's thundering, and the wind has picked up.

"Oh, Sarah, what a wonderful day for a wedding!" Rose says as I bundle her from her front door to my car with my umbrella. At least she doesn't have a delicate train like Ang did, merely a simple, cream satin-and-lace cocktail dress she'd found online.

I'm too busy trying to keep our dresses and my expensive hair style from getting ruined to answer her, but I take a moment to wonder if she's going through a sudden dementia. If she is, it looks good on her because she's glowing.

I pick my way through the damp streets and escort my friend to the back door of the church. Sylvia and Lucia are already in the bridal prep area, dreamy in their dove-gray dresses. They aren't all the same, but they look amazing together. My dress looks great on me, but somehow, I still don't quite fit with Rose's glamorous friends.

It could be the forlorn expression that creeps onto my face whenever I'm not doggedly smiling.

I've tried, I really have. But I've spent the last two weeks basically moping. I miss Sam. I miss Ben. I miss our group. I even miss bratty Brent.

I spoke to Travis about Brent the rodent robber, letting him know what I knew. That seemed like the right thing to do after I asked him to help. Travis appreciated the heads up, but he seemed okay with following through with his offer of assistance so long as Brent follows through with his promise to pay me back.

I wonder if Travis would be so forgiving if he'd already thrown hours of time or several thousand dollars Brent's way. Am I the only one so leery of someone who breaks their word? I can't be, can I?

All I know is, I'm safe from being lied to, but . . . I'm really stinking lonely.

"Ready, girls?" Rose says when her son lets us know we're on. I pull my shoulders back. We've been practicing our moves the last half hour, but I'm nervous.

We begin our slow walk single file down the aisle to the wedding march, but as soon as the music changes to the pop song Rose chose, we break into our moves. I slide sideways, rainbow my arms, shimmy my shoulders, and shake my butt like Damon taught us. I can barely keep up with Lucia and Sylvia, but it's gratifying to see the guests' mouths drop open when we start dancing. After the initial shock, they clap to the beat, smile, and cheer as Rose boogies her way down the aisle.

Charles looks awestruck as we end our thirty-second dance in front of him. He takes Rose's hand and leads her in front of the minister as the guests applaud, and Lucia, Sylvia, and I take our places to one side. I think all weddings should start this way —with joy instead of pomp and circumstance.

Standing up at the front of the chapel as Rose exchanges vows with a dapper Charles, seeing the clear love in their eyes as they whisper to each other and seal their vows with a kiss, and then, later, watching their first dance, I can only wonder dimly— will it ever be my turn?

"Sarah," Charles says after his dance with Rose ends and the band starts a lively big band song. "Will you do this old groom the honor of dancing with him?" He offers me his hand.

I take it. "Of course."

He might be an old groom, but the guy can still cut a rug. He's a strong partner, and I'm breathless halfway through the song from him swinging me around like a rag doll.

"Read any good books lately?" he asks before slinging me away from him and then spinning me back.

I can barely think with my brain sloshing around in my head, but I try to tell him about a fascinating historical mystery I devoured. "It was . . . set in China . . . during the Spanish flu . . . pandemic. In 1918!" He dips me, making me squeal.

"Text me the title. I'll reserve it for when we return from our honeymoon." Unlike Ang and Julian, they're staying local and spending a week at an uber fancy hotel in Vail.

"We're old, and we've seen the world already," Rose told me. "What we want now is to enjoy the time we have together."

I'm thrilled they're going away, because it means I get to take care of Miss Petunia Petalbottom for the week. That dog is going to be spoiled bubblegum pink by the time Rose gets back.

"Charles," I gasp, "I had no idea you were such a . . . wonderful . . . dancer!" I use a short pause in the music to swipe my hair out of my face.

He chuckles as he sweeps me around again. "I have my parents to thank for that. Years of Arthur Murray ballroom dance classes when I was a lad."

"Here's to them!" I shriek as he whirls me around. It's a good thing Charles is holding me when the dance ends or I'd definitely be on my butt, my satin gray bridesmaid dress hitched up to reveal I hadn't had time to replace my ancient Spanx before the wedding.

Charles allows me a moment to recover before taking my hands in his. "Thank you, Sarah, for the dance, for serving as our maid of honor, and most of all, for being a true friend to my Rose. She treasures you, and so, you are also a treasure to me."

Tears jump to my eyes as I hug him. My friends are so ridiculously fortunate. Charles and Julian are real gentleman. All I seem to attract are rats. Lying ones.

I head toward the bar for a glass of water. I've already had some wine and I'm sticking to my one-to-one wine-to-water ratio again tonight. I'm officially on duty, and this MOH won't surrender until the taillights fade on the bride and groom's getaway car.

As I soothe my parched throat, the band finishes a song, and the lead singer asks for everyone's attention.

"With the approval of the bride and groom, one of their guests has a special announcement to make."

I can't see the stage well through the crowd, but when the "guest" speaks into the microphone, I choke. I know that Lie Baby voice all too well.

"Ladies and Gentlemen, forgive the interruption. Let's have a quick round of applause for the reason we're here, Rose and Charles!"

Everyone claps, but as I move cautiously closer to the stage, I see the curious looks the speaker is getting. And I know why— not a single person here knows who the heck he is.

Because it's him. My ex-ex-boyfriend, Ben Becker. I inch as close as I dare, stopping in the shadow of a towering figure where I'm pretty sure that between the man's NBA-sized frame and the lights shining on the stage, Ben can't see me.

What is he doing here? How did he even know when and where the wedding was? Then I remember: I'd sent him the details via text when I'd asked him. I never ever thought he'd actually use them after everything that's happened, but here he is. And oh, my sainted aunt, he looks good enough to eat with the wedding cake fork.

He's wearing a dark suit with a light green tie that I imagine brings out the green in his hazel eyes. His hair is freshly trimmed, and his face is clean shaven. My knees tremble at whatever's about to come out of his mouth.

"My name is Ben Becker. I know not many of you know me and for good reason. I didn't really meet Rose or Charles until, well, a few minutes ago."

The middle-aged couple beside me exchange looks. I don't blame them.

"But I asked Rose for the favor of a few minutes to tell a woman that some of you might know exactly how I feel about her. I was supposed to escort the beautiful and on-point-dancing maid of honor, Sarah Newsome, to the wedding today."

I do my best to melt into the dance floor now, but satin and shoddy Spanx apparently don't melt all that easily.

"I messed up, folks. I told a lie. And although I never meant to deceive Sarah, I did, and it really hurt her. And for that, I'm so terribly sorry."

Ben walks the stage, gesturing and making eye contact with as many guests as he can. Although I'm battling crippling chagrin that he's telling our story to Rose and Charles's entire wedding party and guests, I have to admire his stage presence. I had no idea he was such a showman.

"Sarah, I can't see you," he shades his eyes, "but I really hope you're listening. I came tonight and climbed this stage to speak to you, since you're a difficult woman to catch when you're running away. I need you to know that seeing you again eight weeks ago was like a dream coming true in the basement of the Most Glorious Blood of Christ Church. I didn't know if you'd remember me, if you were still angry with me, or if you'd give me another chance."

He searches the audience for me. I cringe back.

"When you agreed to have coffee with me, you made my week; when you said you'd go on a date with me, you made my month; and when you asked me to be your date for this wedding, you made my year. Now, if you would just do me the tiny favor of forgiving me, you would make my, uh," he scratches his head, "life. Because you're the only woman I want to be with."

He's staring my way as if he can see through the man mountain in front of me.

"Sarah Newsome, give me one more chance, and I promise I'll never need another."

He pauses. A few people that know me spot me hiding and smile and wave me forward encouragingly. I don't budge. I'm muddled, mortified, and I really need to pee.

Ben presses his lips together and nods. "I thought that might not be quite enough." He gestures to the lead singer, who waves to the band, who raise their instruments. Ben takes the microphone in hand. He's going to sing. I had no idea Ben could sing.

"This is by Bryan Adams," he says. "It's called 'Please Forgive Me.'"

He starts into what sounds like a rock ballad all about how he's still holding on, and I'm still the one, and please could I forgive him. At least, I think those are the lyrics. It's hard to focus on the words because Ben is SO. LUDICROUSLY. AWFUL.

I mean, imagine a horse, dog, and goose making a ruckus at the same time, and you have the general idea. Make that a herd of horses, a pack of dogs, and a gaggle of geese.

People around me wince. A few stick their fingers in their ears. One woman stares at Ben, open mouthed, until she actually spills her drink. He doesn't seem to notice or care.

He belts out the song, crooning in the crooning parts, whispering in the whispering parts, pumping his fist in the fist-pumping parts. It's a terrible thing to behold.

I'm so enthralled by his willingness to utterly humiliate

himself in front of hundreds of strangers, that I don't notice Rose slide up next to me. I jump when she takes my arm.

"Oh, Sarah, love, I think he really means it."

"You do?"

She nods. "I do."

The man who's been unwittingly shielding me turns at that and with a groan, says, "Are you Sarah? Please, in the name of all that's good and holy, forgive him and put us out of our misery."

Rose gently pushes me toward the stage. I'm not sure what I'll do, I'm not sure how to feel or what to think. I only know that I need Ben to stop singing right now, before our collective ears bleed.

He doesn't see me in front of the stage at first, mostly because he's bleating the last verse into the microphone, eyes closed. But I can't miss the shine of relief in them when they open, and he recognizes me.

People clap when he finishes, which I'm quite sure is out of giddiness that it's over.

Ben says, "Thank you very much," and hands the microphone back to the real singer. Then, he hops down next to me.

"Sarah, I—"

I touch his lips with my finger. "You've sung, er, said enough. I . . . forgive you."

And at that, he takes me in his arms and kisses me like I've never been kissed before. It shivers me satin-and-Spanx timbers.

The crowd claps again, Ben kisses me again, and the band plays again. For the first time since Sam got sick, all is right in my world.

Again.

Epilogue

Ben

"Are you ready for this?" Julian asks. He must see my clenched jaw, bunched shoulders, and narrowed eyes. I probably look like I'm prepping for a fight instead of walking down a very innocent-looking, flower adorned aisle.

I blink at him. "Is anyone ready for this?"

His face cracks into a grin. "Nope. But somehow, we do it anyway. Probably for them." He tilts his head toward the bride's room down the hall where Sarah, my bride, and her bridesmaids, Ang, Rose, and my soon-to-be sister-in-law Liz, are . . . doing whatever they've been doing in there for two hours.

"Is everything ready?" I ask with a cocked eyebrow.

"If you mean the ring, Adam's taking care of it."

Adam, Julian, and my old friend Jason are my groomsmen. I let out a long breath. "Okay. Good. I can do this."

Julian laughs. "Breathe, man. Breathe and smile, and before you know it, you'll be kissing a beautiful woman, music will be playing, and everyone will be clapping for you. Then, you'll have the rest of your lives together to stress about what you've done."

"That's the part that freaks me out."

He laughs again. I'm glad *he* can be so relaxed. But I've learned over the past two years that nothing much fazes Julian. He's the most chill guy I've ever had the privilege to call my friend. Once Sarah and I started dating after Rose and Charles's blast of a wedding, Julian and I were together a lot, and we got to be tight.

"Thanks for being here." I hold out my hand to clasp his, followed by a chest bump.

Adam hustles in. "We gotta get this show on the road. I'm not sure how long he can make it."

"But it's still a surprise, right?" I say.

"Sarah doesn't have a clue." Adam shakes his head. "I hope you know what you're doing, bro."

I pull a face. "Me, too."

My dad pokes his head in. "You guys ready? They're seating family."

I nod, check my tux and hair one last time in the mirror, and head for the door flanked by Adam and Julian. Adam claps my back.

I stay near the front of the church while Sarah's mom, my folks, and all of our grandparents are seated. My heart's jackhammering and sweat runs like a prison break under my arms.

Sarah and I dated for a year before I popped the question, and then it was another year of dreaming, planning, negotiating, and sometimes arguing to arrive here at the church in June. But somehow, it only feels like a blink since I saw her again at the initial Lost Paws group.

We've kept up a monthly after-party at the Alleycat over the last two years. Sarah and I look forward to it. Out in the pews, I spot Patricia and Raymond, Oscar and Edith, Lydia, Bev, and, at the end of a row, Brent? I thought he was back in jail for violating probation.

When I catch his eye and raise a questioning hand, he flops his lower leg over the side of the pew to show me his ankle monitor.

I give him a thumbs-up.

And then, the music changes to the wedding march. My skin prickles, and I glance at the altar for courage. Here goes. Each step out to my designated spot feels like it takes a million years.

From the front, I watch Julian escort Ang, looking gorgeous in a shimmery navy-blue dress. My friend Jason leads Rose, also beautiful in a similar shade, and Adam guides Sarah's sister Liz, to stand opposite from me. And finally, finally, there's my Sarah.

Seeing her sweeps away all my doubts and fears like dust. Her spectacular dress, the glow of her creamy skin, the love shining in her blue eyes as she finds me at the end of the aisle.

How could I have even one doubt? She's the one. I think I've known it since college, but I had some work to do—on myself—to persuade her.

I step forward to hold her hands in mine, and whisper, "You look incredible."

She beams at me. "You, too. Are you ready?"

"I couldn't be readier."

"Is that a word?" she asks.

"Who cares?"

She turns to face the minister, but I pull her back. "Wait, I have a surprise for you first."

A bark and a whine come from the back of the chapel, and a delighted laugh erupts from the crowd. Sarah's eyes grow huge and watery as a yellow Lab puppy gambols down the aisle. He's all paws, ears, and folds of skin.

When he finally gets to us, I scoop him up. His fur is as soft as fleece, and his breath is pure puppy chow as he tries to lick my cheek.

I untie the bow from around his neck, pull our wedding rings off one end, and hand them to Adam. Sarah pets him gently. "Is he ours?"

I nod.

"But, your allergies—"

We would have gotten a dog long before this if not for them. "I've been secretly getting shots all year. Doc says I should be in good shape."

She nuzzles the puppy, who I haven't named because I knew she'd want to, and then I hand him to Adam, who runs him to our little cousin, Hannah. I'd recruited her to watch him during the ceremony.

A few tears spill onto Sarah's cheeks. "I can't believe I almost didn't give you a second chance, much less a third, Ben Becker. You're wonderful, and I love you." She grins slyly. "Nearly as much as I'm going to love that puppy."

"I love you, too." I pause. "More than anyone or anything in the world."

I take her hand firmly in mine, and together, we face the music—I mean the minister—and grab our happily ever after.

THE END

It all started with a girl, a boy, and a pug named Doug.
Get the exclusive Love & Pets prequel for FREE!
(www.aghenley.com/free-books)

Love & Pets Book 5:
A bitter feud. A burning love. And cats.
Read The Predicament of Persians now!

Read Next

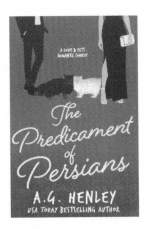

The Predicament of Persians: Love & Pets #5

"What lady is that, which doth enrich the hand of yonder
knight?
- *Romeo and Juliet* (Act 1, Scene 5)

Kathleen

My skin prickles with anticipation as I walk through the lobby of the Hyatt Regency Denver and under the banner hanging overhead that shouts, *Welcome to CatFest*! The logo for the convention has black font on a grass green background with a cat's tail sprouting from the top of the final *t* and underlining the words.

Everywhere I look a clowder of cat lovers mills, sporting things like T-shirts featuring their favorite cartoon cats, rubber kitty noses with whiskers, and plastic claws on their fingers or fake fur tails hanging from belts.

I grab James's arm and squeal. "I can't believe we're finally here!"

"Yeah, it's incredibly exciting," my younger brother deadpans. He puffs a breath of air to blow his hair out of his eyes. His straight, fine, light blonde locks, like a toddler's, fall into his face constantly. I move his bangs to the side so he can see, but he only looks grumpier when the hair slides back again.

James rolls his battered black suitcase in one hand, and he has my Persian cat, Juliet's, carrier in the other. I push my over-sized pink suitcase with a tote bag on top stuffed full of Juliet's food, bowls, grooming equipment, and toothbrush.

"Let's get our keys." I still need to check in for the convention, but first I want to drop my stuff in the room. "I'm sure my poor girl wants out of there, and it's her dinnertime."

"For me, too," my brother says. "You're buying, right? I want room service."

"James, I told you I'd pay all your expenses for coming with me to CatFest. Are you going to ask me if I'm buying every time you want something?"

"Yes." He makes a juvenile face that makes me want to poke him—hard.

I sigh instead. "Just put meals on the room and I'll settle up with you on Sunday when the conference is over." We walk to the reception desk where a petite Latina in her late twenties greets us.

"Checking in for Kathleen Caplin," I say. "I should have a reservation for two nights."

"Yes, ma'am." The agent taps away at her computer keyboard with manicured nails, painted a soft pink.

While she types, I peek in at Juliet. She's looking out at the lobby, her emerald green eyes alert. Her fur, washed and brushed into luxurious perfection this morning before we left, has held up through the two-hour drive from our home in Colorado Springs, the bathroom stop along I-25, and an extended snack break for James.

"Are you okay, beautiful?" I murmur to her. She meows, the sound gentle and pealing, like a delicate bell. As always, her flat face floods my heart with love.

Juliet's fur is white with black tips on her back that give her a silvery appearance. Like most silver chinchilla Persians, her brick red nose has a black outline. She also has the large, bright green eyes that seem to droop just a bit, giving her a sad kitty look. Her gorgeous looks are why we're here. Juliet is my Instagram CelebriCat and hundreds of people are coming to the con this weekend to meet her, including a representative from Purina's sponsorship program.

The agent glances at my brother. "And do you have a reservation, sir?"

"You got me my own room, right?" James asks me in a loud voice.

I wince and hand the agent my credit card. "No, James, we're sharing."

"What?" He drops a hand on the desk with a sharp smack. "Sharing wasn't part of the deal."

The agent stares, open-mouthed, at my brother. He only has one volume when he's annoyed—earsplitting. I put a hand on his arm and lower my voice.

"James, the rooms were over three-hundred dollars a night. I could only afford one."

He groans. "I hope the room at least has a big tub."

"I'm sure it does." I speak through gritted teeth. Oh, how I wish I didn't know how much my brother likes his baths.

With a hesitant smile, and another sidelong glance at James, the agent hands me a small folder with two keycards inside. "Your room is on the twelfth floor. The elevators are just there, to the left." She points the way.

"You have room service, right?" James asks her.

"Yes, sir, of course."

"Then, I want a BLT with fries and a beer."

Her eyes dart to me, and I infuse as much apology as I can into my expression. Down the desk, a man checking in seems to be listening. He can hardly help it, thanks to James. His own desk agent keeps snatching glances at us, too.

The eavesdropper's hair color captures my eye. It's almost the exact same shade as mine—deep red with gold highlights. But his skin is bronzed, like he lives somewhere much warmer year-round than Colorado. His full mouth and his cornflower blue eyes curl up with amusement. I smile apologetically at him, too, and then turn back to my agent. After a flustered pause, she seems to be trying to come up with a polite response to my brother.

"Um, yes sir, if you'll just pick up the phone in your room and push the in-room dining button, you'll be able to order from our extensive menu of—"

James grunts. "What kind of place is this? I can't order room service at the desk?"

I grip his forearm and speak to the woman, who looks completely flustered. "We'll do that, thank you so much."

With an aghast glance at the handsome ginger-haired man, I grab my wallet and the key cards and push James and all our stuff along in front of me.

I bend down to whisper in my brother's ear, grateful for my five feet eleven inches. It gives me a tiny bit of authority. "Can you please not be rude to everyone in the hotel this weekend? This conference means a lot to me."

As he well knows. He grunts again. "Whatever. I'm hungry."

My limbs feel stiff with humiliation as I march toward the elevators. Why didn't I have a *normal* brother? Why did I get an oversized child? James has been the downfall of so many of my plans over the years, but with our parents gone, no one else will put up with him.

Even though the elevator button is already lit, my brother uses his elbow to bang it an extra five times, drawing looks from a couple waiting to go upstairs. They wear matching shirts with one giant cat face on them—looks like a tabby with the "M" on the forehead split between them. The woman wears the left side of the cat's face, and the man wears the right.

James looks them up and down and shakes his head. "Bunch of crazy cat lovers. I'll bet you all have mad-cat disease."

I close my eyes to avoid their justifiably offended stares. How can I already regret bringing him to CatFest when we haven't even gotten to our room yet?

❦

"Go, girl, seek happy nights to happy days."
- *Romeo and Juliet* (Act 1, Scene 3)

Kathleen

One hour, and one tense exchange with a disgruntled room service waiter later, I escape from the hotel room.

James had called the poor man at least five times to tell him to hurry up while I was changing clothes and freshening my makeup in the bathroom, and then he'd refused to put on pants to answer the door when the food came. James always takes his pants off the moment he gets home, and hotel rooms are no different. I'd ended up answering the door and getting the tray. James would have scared the guy half to death; he hasn't bought new underwear in about ten years.

Before I leave, I make sure Juliet has food and water and that her litter box is set up. She and James are curled up watching My Cat from Hell on the television while the last bloody bites of a rare burger and a few forlorn fries stare at me from the ketchup smeared plate beside him.

Is there a show called My Brother from Hell? I could write, produce, and star in it with one hand tied behind my back. I kiss Juliet on the head while James bats my hair out of his face so he can see.

"I'm going to the hotel bar for a drink," I tell him. He grunts. A grunt is one of his favorite replies.

I breathe deeply, calming myself and my blood pressure, as I stand in front of the elevator door. The mirror on the wall to my side, hanging over a fake potted plant, shows me that the few extra minutes I took to primp had paid off. My wavy, waist-length hair frames my pale face, and a magenta leather jacket pops against my light-wash denim jeans. Fringed pink ankle boots top off—or bottom off—the outfit. I feel good, ready to meet some other cat lovers and have a good time. Without James.

The Peaks Lounge is on the twenty-seventh floor of the hotel with spectacular views of downtown Denver and the Rocky Mountains to the west. The sun sinks slowly toward the foothills but still casts a beautiful glow. I step to the window to admire the panorama and then turn to find somewhere to sit.

People cram the place and clearly most are here for the convention. It's not hard to tell. They wear cat pajamas, cat onesies, necklaces with cats as pendants, pants with tiny cat silhouettes on them, and at least one pair of furry orange cat slippers. I'd read they're expecting over twenty-thousand convention-goers this year. I slip on my own pair of sleek black cat ears from my bag and relax for the first time since I got James in the car almost three hours ago. These are my people.

A barstool opens up, and I slip onto it. The female bartender, a woman in her mid-twenties with purple streaks in her braided hair, pushes a menu in front of me before hurrying off.

Oh, how cute. They're offering cat themed drinks especially for CatFest. When the barkeep returns, I order a Kitty Royale, which promises to be both delicious and a deep pink. Then, I check Juliet's Instagram account, @julietcatulet.

A direct message waits for me from one of her fans who goes by the Instagram account name of @pigletandpink. I know from previous exchanges the person is actually two women. They ask what time I'll be in the lounge. I type quickly that I'm here and what I look like. I don't ever post pictures of myself on Juliet's account. She's the star; I'm only her manager. And stage crew, costumer, producer, and purchasing agent.

I peer around, and spot two women headed my way who stop a couple feet away.

"Hey! Are you Juliet's owner?" One of the women, a curvy Latina, asks me. She has black hair to her waist, tattoos, and multiple piercings in her ears, eyebrows, nose, and lips.

I twist in my stool to stand and greet them. "Yes, I'm Kathleen. Are you Piglet or Pink?" I hold out my hand, but the woman who spoke grabs me in a bear hug instead of shaking it.

"Piglet! Good to finally meet you. I'm Viviana, but you can call me Viv. And this is my girlfriend, Jess." I shake Jess's hand, too. She's Asian, has equally long hair, and exactly one dainty hoop eyebrow ring. I'm guessing she's Pink; her hair is a vivid shade of flamingo.

These women are Catulets, what Juliet's most loyal fans and supporters call themselves. They often jump in to defend her when that hateful Romeo Meowtague leaves snarky comments on my posts.

"I love your account," I say. "Thanks so much for always supporting Juliet and me."

I've gotten used to my cat's sometimes unusual fans. They're men and women of all ages and from all walks of life. They don't even all seem to be cat owners, although most probably are.

Piglet and Pink are visual artists who happen to really love cats. Their apartment looks like a rainbow exploded across the walls, and they have a maelstrom of mousers.

"Are you excited for the meet and greet tomorrow?" Jess asks.

"Yes! I just hope Juliet cooperates."

"She's going to do great," Viv says. "She seems like such a love. We can't wait to meet her."

"You're coming?" I ask.

"We wouldn't miss it. And we have a few things to say to Romeo's owner. That twit," Jess adds. "Did you see his latest comment on your pre-convention post?"

"No, I haven't had a chance to read them." Typically, comments take a while to read through. I usually get hundreds after I post. When a cat has over one million fans, every post tends to get plenty of attention.

I open the app again. My last post was of Juliet with her miniature long blonde wig and a spring green silk dress on. She's lying on a low cat couch that I had covered in gold taffeta and a tiny suitcase sits beside her. For the caption, I'd written:

"My horse, my horse! My kingdom for a horse!" - *Richard III* (Act 5, Scene 4) Juliet's ready for #CatFestDenver! See you there!

My cat's stage name of Juliet Catulet is a variation on the famous Shakespearean character, Juliet Capulet, of course. I scroll down and spot the comment right away. My lips thin.

romeo.meowtague: See you at #CatFestDenver #IGCelebriCat meet and greet tomorrow. Let the best cat win. Which will be me, of course.

I shake my head. "He's such a jerk." My gaze slides around the bar. "He could be here right now. I don't know what he looks like, do you?"

Viv shrugs and shakes her head. "But you're right. He's *so* rude." She pats my shoulder. "Don't worry, the Catulets have your back. We'll make sure Juliet wins Best Newcomer tomorrow night. We've all voted."

I swallow hard and smile gratefully at them. "I hope you're

right. You two did a great job getting the word out about the award."

Jess pulls her hair over her shoulder. "Juliet has it in the bag. Listen, we're headed to dinner. We'll see you tomorrow at the meet and greet."

I consider asking if I can join them as Viv takes Jess's hand. It would be fun to hang out with fans, but I chicken out.

Viv waves. "Have a good night and make sure you and Juliet get your beauty rest." They wind through the tables and out of the lounge.

I sigh and read through the post comments. Several Catulets have commented on Juliet's account to say they can't wait to meet her tomorrow or Sunday at the official Instagram Cele-briCat meet and greets. I type out enthusiastic responses, and then I respond to Romeo's owner.

julietcatulet: @romeo.meowtague Whatever. Go hide under a rock. I'm the feline queen and everyone knows it. #Cat-FestDenver #IGCelebriCat #julietforbestnewbie

Several fans pipe in quickly, backing me up. I know it's childish to fight like this. Part of me means what I say, and part of me panders to my fans, who seem to love Romeo and Juliet's catfights. The fact that the cats, or at least their owners, are not only clearly *not* in love, but actively feud, seems to delight them more.

For fun, and only after I'd realized Juliet loved it, I'd started taking pictures of her in handmade silk or satin medieval dresses and posting them on Instagram with Shakespearean quotes as captions. As her fandom grew, I'd posed her on my porch swing in the moonlight or with James dressed as her Nurse. Which I'd paid him well for and which he'd hated doing. Which had made me want to do it more often.

The more Shakespearean posts I'd created for Juliet's account, the more her fame had grown. After a particularly well liked-and-shared post six months ago, she'd gone viral. Now, incredibly, she has a million and a half followers. I created a few pieces of Juliet Catulet merchandise like T-shirts and mugs to sell online and the first batch sold in less than a day.

Other than the meet and greets tomorrow and Sunday, Juliet and I have a dinner and awards ceremony tomorrow night. Well, I have the dinner and awards ceremony. Cats aren't allowed. And finally, I'm meeting a Purina representative about sponsorship over breakfast on Sunday morning. I shiver with excitement.

If things go well tomorrow night, and Juliet wins the Best Newcomer award that she's nominated for, then I might be able to 1) work fewer hours at the hair salon where I currently slave away six days a week, 2) build a real business around Juliet's success, and 3) get James his own apartment.

James needs to get his own place. Yesterday. The Purina sponsorship could be his ticket to adulting and mine to freedom.

A notification appears on my phone, and my mood sours. It's another comment from Romeo. I mean, not really. After all, Romeo Meowtague is a cat—a very handsome black Persian cat with copper colored eyes and a self-assured expression. The comment is from his horrible owner, whom I've never met, or even seen, but assume must be male due to his smarmy arrogance.

romeo.meowtague: @julietcatulet The queen of what? Just curious #romeorules

julietcatulet: @romeo.meowtague You, for one thing. Obviously. #julietforbestnewbie

romeo.meowtague: @julietcatulet Snort. Please, queen, spare me. We'll settle this once and for all tomorrow night. #romeorules

I make a scornful sound.

Romeo's owner and I have feuded since he'd showed up one day on the Instagram scene and stole my Shakespeare theme, trying to horn in on Juliet's fame. He dresses Romeo in little doublets or blousy shirts and tights with wooden swords next to him and the occasional vial of fake poison.

He'd direct messaged me early on about a collaboration. It

had made a certain sense, joining the accounts of feline Juliet and Romeo. But on top of stealing my theme, he'd been so pushy and unprofessional about it, sending me repeated DMs when I hadn't responded right away and never telling me his real name, that I'd soured on the idea almost immediately. We'd gone back and forth for a while before I'd finally said no. I'm not going to partner with an arrogant copycat, no matter how clever his name.

After I'd rejected his advances, Romeo's owner had started leaving these kinds of nasty comments on Juliet's account. At first, I'd ignored them. When the comments had become more pointed, I'd tried messaging him to cease and desist. I'd been formal, but nice. When he still hadn't stopped, I'd blocked him.

But—and I'm not very proud of this—Juliet's page had better engagement by allowing Romeo and his Meowtagues to comment. The Catulets love the bickering, and the feud had helped grow both of our followings. So, I'd unblocked him and reengaged.

But I absolutely cannot stand the man. And I plan to tell him that in no uncertain terms when I finally meet him tomorrow.

As I'm scrolling through comments, someone touches my arm. I look up and my heart lurches. It's the handsome redheaded man from the desk, smiling down at me.

"Excuse me," he says. "Will you shake my hand? I want to tell my friends I've been touched by an angel."

Read The Predicament of Persians: Love & Pets #5 now!

Acknowledgments

I wasn't so sure I should write this book. I didn't know if I could pull off even a mildly humorous book about a pet grief support group. But in the end, I loved every minute of it. The book spoke to two important sides of my personality: the pet lover who has lived through the grief of losing a beloved animal and the professional psychologist.

I have run therapy groups myself, and I'm always amazed by how they come together despite starting with a room full of perfect strangers. I'm awed by how the group dynamics affect the sessions, how the group members work to help each other as well as themselves, and how as the therapist, you sometimes have to hang on tight while the group runs itself in directions you never expected. The Lost Paws group was no exception, and they're close to my heart now.

The Henley Huddle is another wonderful group in my life. They're my team of Advanced Readers who elect to receive a free copy of my books and often choose to leave an honest review of them at the release. Thank you for your enthusiasm, Huddle - you're the best! While we're at it, I'm so grateful to all of my readers. Your reviews, your notes of encouragement, and your visits on social media make this writing job even more fun.

Many thanks to Najla Qamber of Najla Qamber Designs for this series's adorable covers, and to Krista Dapkey of KD Proofreading. If you need a quick, friendly, and professional proofreader, she's your woman.

And, always and forever, thank you to my friends and family for your steady support and love.

Also by A. G. Henley

The Love & Pets Series (Sweet Romantic Comedy)

Love, Pugs, and Other Problems: A Love & Pets Prequel Story

The Problem with Pugs

The Trouble with Tabbies

The Downside of Dachshunds

The Lessons of Labradors

The Predicament of Persians

The Conundrum of Collies

The Pandemonium of Pets: A Love & Pets Christmas Romance

The Love & Pets Series Box Set: Books 1 - 3

ॐ

Nicole Rossi Thrillers (Young Adult)

Double Black Diamond

ॐ

The Brilliant Darkness Series (Young Adult Fantasy)

The Scourge

The Keeper: A Brilliant Darkness Story

The Defiance

The Gatherer: A Brilliant Darkness Story

The Fire Sisters

The Brilliant Darkness Boxed Set

ॐ

Novellas (Young Adult Fantasy)

Untimely

Featured in *Tick Tock: Seven Tales of Time*

Basil and Jade

Featured in *Off Beat: Nine Spins on Song*

The Escape Room

Featured in *Dead Night: Four Fits of Fear*